HUTCH

AUTHOR

SUSIE MCIVER

HUTCH
SEAL SECURITY BOOK 6

**AUTHOR
SUSIE MCIVER**

Copyright © 2023 by Susie McIver Author

All rights reserved.

No part of this publication may be reproduced, distributed, or transmitted in any form or by any means, including photocopying, recording, or other electronic or mechanical methods, without the prior written permission of the publisher, except as permitted by U.S. copyright law. For permission requests, contact [include publisher/author contact info].

The story, all names, characters, and incidents portrayed in this production are fictitious. No identification with actual persons (living or deceased), places, buildings, and products is intended or should be inferred.

Book Cover by Amanda Walker

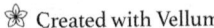 Created with Vellum

HUTCH CAMPBELL
THIS WAS THEN

I paused and scanned the room. I was finally a Navy SEAL. My heart was racing with excitement. I was so damn excited, I looked at my buddies. We all graduated together: Leo Hudson, Mace Cohen, Blade Wilder, and Gabe Steller, Jackson Barlow was around here somewhere. It wouldn't surprise me if he hasn't already found himself someone soft to spend the night with. We had grown up together and knew what we wanted to do after graduating college. My brother Gray also had dreams of becoming a SEAL. But my mother wasn't thrilled about it. Nevertheless, we worked tirelessly to achieve our dream and tonight, we planned to celebrate.

We heard that women loved Navy SEAL officers, and I was looking forward to spending time with a particular server I had seen at the club last night. I didn't know her name, but I planned to find out, before the night was over.

"Hey, Hutch, are you daydreaming, or are we going to party all night?" Leo asked.

"Let's party all night. I'll call an Uber," I replied, glancing over at my brother who wasn't a SEAL.

"Are you coming with us Gray?"

"Only if you tell the ladies I'm your Lieutenant."

"You got it, Lieutenant. Just don't try to steal my lady friend," I said with a chuckle.

"Hey big brother, point her out to me and I'll stay away from her. But don't be surprised if I find myself someone."

"Just don't go out with any of the women Grandma sets you up with. Trust me I learned that the hard way," I warned.

"What are you talking about? Grandma always tries to set me up with strange women I don't know."

"She set me up with Beatrice Price. I couldn't believe it when I saw her at the restaurant. We don't like each other. We haven't since I was in the fifth grade, and she slammed the door shut on my fingers."

"Hutch, Bea felt terrible about that, and you know it. My God, she was in the third grade. She apologized to you so many times. Why have you held it against her for so long? You two were friends."

"She laughed at me. I turned around to see who slammed the door, and she was laughing.

"I doubt she was laughing at you. She's not that kind of person. Besides, she apologized a hundred times, that day. You should give her a chance."

"Then you go out with her. I don't still blame Beatrice for that damn door. It's just that I don't know how to talk to her, after the way I acted." I left out the part about me dreaming about her, she's so damn hot.

"I asked her out she refused."

"You asked Beatrice out on a date?"

"Yes. Why not? She's beautiful."

"I don't want to talk about Beatrice Price," I said scanning the room for the hot server. Then I saw her across the room, waiting on some guys.

Mace passed around the beers and spoke. "I went out with her." I would have taken her out again, but I mentioned the incident, and she got angry. She said you were the biggest baby she had ever known. Then she got up and walked out of the restaurant."

"Are you talking about my Beatrice? I can't believe you dated her. You knew how I felt about her. Why have you guys always called it the incident?"

"Because you never wanted to hear anything about it, you would start screaming like a baby. Besides, she is not your Beatrice."

"I didn't act like a baby. Besides, I'm lucky I could use my fingers after that injury."

Gray, spit beer; he laughed so hard. "Oh, please, your hand hurt for two days. It's not like it lasted years."

"I agree with Gray. Not only is Bea nice, but she's also hotter than hell."

"I took a long drink of my beer. *I knew how hot Beatrice was. I've watched her growing up for years. Hell, she lived across the street from us. I knew she was away at college. She wanted to be a doctor.* Honestly, I don't know why I acted as I did. I tried to tell her I wasn't mad anymore. She slugged me in the stomach. After that, I stopped talking to her. "Damn, we are here to party—no more about Beatrice."

"Are you guys talking about the incident?" Blade asked, sitting down.

"No, we are finished talking about that. I'm going to see when that beauty gets off work and see if she wants company for the night." I walked back to our table with a grin.

My brother smiled. "I take it she said yes. Is that safe? Screwing someone you don't know?"

"Shut the fuck up. You are not ruining my night." They busted out laughing. I knew they set me up for that one."

"I have to go," Mace said, killing his beer. "I'm meeting Cindy. We have our own celebration to do."

"See you in a couple of days."

BEATRICE
THIS WAS THEN

BEATRICE PRICE

I kicked off my shoes and sank into a chair. My feet were killing me after a long day at medical school. But I knew it would be tough, so I was prepared for anything. Working in the ER all night had been especially stressful, but it was all worth it. I couldn't wait to become a pediatrician and have my own practice someday.

My break was over, and I got back up to work. Just then an ambulance rushed in a heart attack victim. When I walked into the cubical, I recognized the man immediately. This was Hutch's father. They lived across the street from us. We worked on him for a long time.

I looked over at Doctor Johnson. We went to school together. He was always with the Campbell brothers. My mind flashed to Hutch Campbell. I haven't spoken to him since I was in the third or fourth grade. I knew everything he's done with his life. I mean, he was the popular kid in school. Now he was a Navy Seal.

I went into the waiting room. Mrs. Campbell and Jenny,

Hutch's sister, were crying. I sat down and quietly talked to them. I explained to them everything that was going on with Mr. Campbell. I told them how bad the heart attack was and that they might want to call the boys to be with them.

I was still shocked when I walked into the hospital two days later and ran into Hutch Campbell. He was more handsome than I remembered. I never knew he was as big as he was. His shoulders were broad, and he was gorgeous. As I bumped into him, my hand brushed against his chest, which felt as hard as a rock, I felt a sudden rush of attraction. My hand may have lingered longer than necessary. *He must work out all the time.*

I saw him working in his yard when he came back from college. He was always distant with me, whereas he was friendly and approachable with others. I reminded myself that I wasn't a child anymore and that my feelings shouldn't get hurt. I saw him watching me a few times, like he wanted to say something.

"Excuse me, I said, turning away from him."

"Beatrice, are you my father's doctor?" he asked.

"No, I'm working in the emergency room. I just wanted to see how your dad is doing?" I realized I was standing too close to him, and his scent was intoxicating. It wasn't safe for me to be this close.

I had forgotten to mention earlier that I had secretly been in love with Hutch Campbell since I was in the third grade when we were friends, until I accidentally slammed the door on his hand. Now here he was, frowning at me again.

"Why don't you tell us how he is? We can't get any information out of anyone else. So, Beatrice, please tell us how my father is doing."

Hutch is the only one I know who calls me Beatrice, and I know he does it because he's still angry about the door incident. I refused to let him get under my skin. I turned to see who else was in the room. Gray and Jenny were there with their mom. I sat down next to Jenny and her mom I took Mrs. Campbell's hand.

"Your husband's heart is plum tuckered out. He won't get any better after he leaves the hospital. He might have a few months to live. This was his third and most severe heart attack. It was just too much. So, when he goes home, he needs to be kept comfortable. Do you have any questions?

"I do."

I knew Hutch was going to say something. I turned to face him. "What do you want to know?"

"First, I wanted to tell you that I'm sorry I acted like a jerk to you for all these years. I was stupid and immature. It wasn't your fault the door closed on my hand. You were just a small child, and I was an ass. I'm sorry. When can Dad go home?"

I was stunned. After all these years, he finally apologized for treating me badly. *I have to admit he told me he was sorry before, but I ignored it.*

I wiped away a stupid tear that escaped from my eye. "Probably tomorrow. You might want to hire a nurse to help him. He'll be able to move around, but if he experiences any pressure on his heart, it could trigger another attack. You don't want him to become breathless. That causes the heart to work faster. We don't want that to happen."

Hutch nodded, and I looked at the others. Gray was watching his brother, and I think he was surprised Hutch apologized to me in front of the others. I know I was. "Okay then, I'll see you later." I got up and walked out of the room.

Mr. Campbell went home two days later. I went about my business with a secret smile because Hutch finally apologized to me and he was a grown up, plus he smelled so good. *I was pathetic.*

1

HUTCH
THIS IS NOW.

As I carefully sanded down the weathered wooden boat, my attention was inadvertently drawn to my brother Gray's conversation about a brawl between two people. According to him, Beatrice Price had apparently gotten into a fight with Willy Freeman, and the details rapidly spread through our little town Cedar Falls, Oregon. But what really caught my attention was when Gray revealed that Beatrice was highly skilled in martial arts. How had I never known about this?

I wiped my rag across the beautiful wood on the boat. Gray and Gilly planned to keep this boat for themselves. My muscles throbbed from the hours I had dedicated working on the boat whenever an opportunity arose. "Did I hear you correctly? Beatrice Price was involved in a fight with Willy Freeman?" I inquired.

"Yep, that's the talk on the streets," Gray affirmed.

"Who told you?" I asked.

"Gilly told me. She took the baby in for a check-up and saw Bea with a swollen, painful-looking black eye. When

Gilly asked what happened, Bea claimed that Willy Freeman had sucker punched her."

"What the hell. Why did he punch her," I demanded to know.

"I figured it was connected with his little boy as I, said before, Beatrice Price is a blackbelt in martial arts. I'm sure Willy had more than a black eye," Gray speculated.

"No, I had no idea that she was trained in martial arts," I said, genuinely surprised. "When did she have time to take classes to become an expert in anything besides her medical profession?"

"Don't you remember we used to attend her karate class but quit because we didn't find it enjoyable?" Gray reminded me.

"Why are you getting upset?" Gilly asked, looking at me with concern.

"I'm not upset," I said.

"But you're sanding a hole in that piece of wood. Does this have something to do with that incident you told me about? she asked Gray.

"You told her how stupid I was as a kid?" I asked.

"Not just as a kid," Gray said.

"I don't know why I acted the way I did. Yes, I do. It was because that little girl laughed at me, and my hand was throbbing in pain. I had forgotten that Beatrice laughed when she felt nervous or scared. I'm sure she was frightened because I screamed at her. I'm ashamed of myself," Hutch admitted.

"Plus, he apologized to Bea, and she never accepted his apology."

"How do you know she didn't accept his apology?" Gilly inquired.

"Because she still won't talk to him. Bea bought her

parent's house, after they retired and moved to Miami. Her home is across the street from my mom's house."

"I aware of all of that." Gilly retorted.

"It's possible that she's so accustomed to Hutch ignoring her and feeling embarrassed that she seeks refuge at home to protect herself," Gilly said. "I'm certain that's the reason."

"That's it. She's protecting herself from being hurt," I stood up to leave. "I have to go."

"Where are you headed?" Gilly inquired.

"I'm going to talk to Beatrice. I need to make things right."

Gilly looked at me like I was crazy. "But she's at the hospital today."

I nodded and left. Ten minutes later, I entered the hospital and saw Cassie, Luca's wife.. "Where is the children's floor?"

"Second floor. Why are you here?" Cassie inquired.

"When did you start working here?" I said instead of answering her.

"After I helped Griff with Tag's surgery, I had to start working here. I have to give them ten months. So here I am. Now tell me why you are here?"

"I'm looking for Beatrice Price."

"Oh, really, I thought the two of you hadn't spoken since the incident," Cassie remarked.

"Goodbye." *Did I hear her giggle?* I took the stairs. As soon as I entered the children's floor, I was greeted by the sound of Beatrice's laughter. It was unmistakable, having heard it in the company of my sister Jenny. Guided by the sound, I stood in the doorway of a child's room, where I witnessed Doctor Beatrice Price engaging with a sick toddler, bringing joy to the child's face.

Turning her head, she frowned at my presence. She

kissed the child and said something to the nurse, and walked out of the room. "Can I help you? Is there something wrong?" She inquired, her gaze locking with mine.

"Caught off guard by her mesmerizing aquamarine eyes, I struggled to gather my thoughts." She was undeniably beautiful. I forced myself to avert my gaze. "Beatrice, I want to express my profound apologies for the way I treated you. I was stupid not only during my childhood but also during all the years when I acted like a complete ass. I'm sorry for everything."

"You've already apologized," she replied calmly.

"I know, but I wasn't certain if you truly believed me," I confessed.

"Why would you think I wouldn't believe you," she questioned.

"Because whenever I drive to my mom's house, you leave and walk home. It made me question if you truly accepted my apology."

"I'm sorry I don't have time to talk now. I did accept your apology. If I leave when you show up, it's because I don't want to make either of us uncomfortable. The entire town knows about that damn incident, and frankly, I have no desire to revisit those old wounds. If you will excuse me, I have children to attend to," she explained, turning away and leaving me momentarily breathless. I stood there, dumbfounded. Why had I come to the hospital? Was I acting irrationally when it came to Beatrice?

SWEAT TRICKLED down my neck and chest, and arm-pits dampening my dirty tee shirt, emblazoned with the words, "I like them big-breasted." Unless she saw the back of the shirt, she wouldn't realize it referred to turkeys. I ran my hand through my hair. It was too long and curled as it tended to do when it needed to be cut.

I looked around, and Lucy, Adam Wilson's wife and Gilly's sister stood there watching me. She shook her head at me; damn, why did she have to be at work today. Great, now she would probably tell Gilly everything I said. Then unexpectedly, she approached me.

"It might have been better if you had waited until she got home to talk to her. She might think your feelings are hurt and be worried about that. It's best to have a private conversation when there aren't too many people around." Lucy advised me.

"My feelings aren't hurt," I said, frowning.

"That's okay if they are. We'll talk later," Lucy responded; I could see pity on her face.

"I'm telling you, my feelings aren't hurt," I said, trying to get her to believe me.

"I know. That's okay." Lucy reassured me before turning and walking into a room. What the fuck just happened? Why did she think my feelings were hurt? Damn, she's Gilly's sister; she's probably already on the phone, spreading the news that poor Hutch got his feelings hurt. I need to get the hell out of here before someone else sees me.

I was in the elevator when I unexpectedly ran into Doctor Jack Johnson, my brother-in-law.

"Hutch, is something wrong? Why are you here?" Jack asked with concern.

"Everything is fine. I just dropped by to see what you're doing this weekend. I wanted to know if you might want to go fishing," I quickly responded.

"Oh, you want to go fishing. I didn't know you liked fishing. I would love to, but I'm on call this weekend. How come you didn't call me?" Jack questioned.

"I actually forgot my phone," I lied, relieved that I had left it in the truck. As soon as the elevator doors opened, I swiftly exited.

Jack chuckled. "You are on the maternity floor, Hutch."

"Fuck," I cursed internally. "I'm taking the stairs. See you around." I turned and was gone before he could say another word. *I am so frigging stupid for coming here.*

2

BEATRICE

Goodness, that man is frigging gorgeous. His eyes make me want to shed my clothes and have my way with him. He smells so good. I wanted to move in closer and cuddle with him. The heat radiating from his body was so intense. I swear my body is trembling, standing next to him. Now I understand why I always leave when he's around.

I don't want him to see how strongly I'm drawn to him. How can I be attracted to someone who bullied me as a child." Well, not actually—bullied, more like he ignored me. I've said it before, but I can't help but feel pathetic when it comes to Hutch Campbell. I was lost in those beautiful Gray eyes of his.

I walked into the bathroom, running cold water on my hands and wrist, trying to forget my reaction to him.

"Hello, Doctor Price," Lucy greeted me.

"Lucy, I told you to call me Bea," I reminded her.

"Not while we are at the hospital. You deserve to be addressed as Doctor. You've worked hard to earn that title," she replied before changing the subject. "I spoke to Hutch, poor thing. I think his feelings were hurt."

I nearly choked on my laughter upon hearing that. My eyes watered as I laughed. "Let me tell you something, Hutch Campbell never gets his feelings hurt. He's usually the one causing the pain. That's why I stay out of his way."

"But that was such a heartfelt apology."

"Yes, it was, but it was twenty-five years too late. I'm sorry. I won't talk about Hutch," I replied, suppressing my amusement, although I couldn't deny the truth of how I really felt about Hutch. *Only in the solitude of my thoughts and the privacy of my shower do I allow myself to dwell on him. Truly, I am pathetic.*

"I apologize. I won't mention him again," Lucy said sincerely.

"Thank you," I dried my hands and left. How typical that Lucy overheard our conversation, considering she's Gilly's sister and Gilly is married to Hutch's brother Grayson. I didn't want to sound unkind, but I never discussed Hutch.

"Thank you," I dried my hands and left. How typical that Lucy overheard our conversation, considering she's Gilly's sister and Gilly is married to Hutch's brother, Grayson. I didn't mean to sound unkind, but after the pain Hutch Campbell caused me, I couldn't risk exposing that little eight-year-old girl to harm once again.

I pushed any thoughts of Hutch aside as I focused on the remainder of my shift. There was simply no time to dwell on anything. Oh, Beatrice Rose Price, who are you trying to fool? Hutch Campbell, I couldn't risk putting that little eight-year-old girl in harm's way again. I didn't think about Hutch as I worked the rest of my shift. I was too busy to dwell on anything. *Beatrice Rose Price, who are you lying to?*

Why does he want me to accept his apology? He's never

come looking for me before. Does he feel guilty for how he has treated me all these years? Good, I hope he does feel guilty. He deserves to feel something. I pushed those few times he had already apologized to me out of my head. Where the hell did he get that tee shirt? Big-breasted? He's not in college anymore, so throw the shirt away, for Christ's sake.

When I left the hospital, it was well past midnight. My hunger led me to Burger King, where I ordered a large chicken sandwich and a milkshake. When I pulled into my garage, I thought I saw a light in the back bedroom turn off. My parents must have come for a visit. I opened the door to the kitchen and walked inside. "Mom, are you guys here?"

A noise caught my attention, followed by the sound of something shattering. I cautiously made my way toward the back of the house. A chill ran down my spine as I discovered some of my belongings scattered on the floor. I backed up to leave, realizing someone was in my house. I ran back to the kitchen and grabbed my purse to get my phone.

I dialed nine-one-one. "Someone is in my house," I quickly provided my address, "I don't know how many," Suddenly, a knife whizzed past my head. I screamed and dropped my phone. Two men menacingly stared at me and burst into laughter. Although I believed I could win in a fight, the thought of hurting someone never crossed my mind. Nevertheless, I would do whatever it took to save my own life.

As one of the attackers charged at me, I swiftly delivered a powerful kick to his gut, propelling him backward. The other assailant came at me, but I successfully employed the same move to knock him down. However, he anticipated my actions and managed to grab hold of my foot. Fortunately, I skillfully twisted free from his grasp. Both men renewed their assault, but my martial arts training instinctively kicked in, enabling me to defend myself. Having practiced martial arts since the age of five, I knew what I was doing, although I had never before used it in a real-life situation. I felt relieved that my training proved effective.

One of the attackers swung at me. As I heard the approaching sirens, I made a dash for the front door. However, before I could escape, one of the men grabbed me from behind, pulling my hair. Suddenly, a fierce roar resonated through the room, and the next moment, the attacker vanished.

Turning around, I saw both assailants sprawled unconscious on the floor, while a man stood before me, seemingly unfazed, as if such encounters were a regular part of his life. His muscles rippled, he was shirtless, and his sweats hung low on his hips. I couldn't help but notice the absence of tan lines.

"You should have called me first," he remarked, addressing me.

"How could I have done that when I don't have your phone number?"

"I'll give it to you."

"I don't want your phone number. Excuse me, I need to talk to the police," I said, closing my eyes and turning around. "Thank you, Hutch, for saving me," I added, knowing that I would have been able to defend myself but appreciating his help nonetheless.

"You're welcome," he responded.

As I spoke to the police Hutch stood faithfully by my side, like a watchdog ready to attack anyone who said the wrong thing. I could sense his presence the entire time he stood there. Heat radiated from his body to mine. Eventually, the attackers were soon whisked away in a police car, and I went back inside to hunt for my food. When I turned around, Hutch was still there, watching me.

"Would you like to split my chicken sandwich?"

"Yes, please," he accepted. I cut the sandwich in half and shared my milkshake with him. He was much larger than me, so I gave him the bigger portion of the sandwich and shake.

"Why are you here so late at night? Is your mom okay?" I inquired, attempting to strike up a conversation.

Taking a bite of my sandwich, I observed my unexpected guest. Talking with Hutch felt peculiar, and twice in one day was really strange. As he devoured his portion of the sandwich along with his shake, Hutch reminded me of one of those men on the front of a romance book, a Hot Navy SEAL, with his sculpted physique.

Not to mention his bare chest and sweats that barely hung on his hips. My eyes followed the hairline until it disappeared into his pant line. No one should have to stand next to this beautiful body without at least getting to run her hands across his chest. *I'll say it again, I'm pathetic.*

"Why are you around here so late at night? Is your mom okay?" I inquired, attempting to start a conversation.

"I'm painting Mom's kitchen. Adam Wilson called me and said a call came in from you about someone in your house. So here I am," he explained.

"Yes, so here you are," I acknowledged, feeling a tinge of strangeness. "We've only heard each other's voices a few times in all these years, and now we've spoken twice in one day."

"I've heard your voice before, he admitted."

"You have? When?"

"Just here and there in high school," he elaborated.." Will you ever forget how horrible I was?"

"Can I ask you why you want me to forget it?"

"For most of those years, I forgot I was being so horrible because I'd been away for so long since I was eighteen. When I finally realized my behavior, I couldn't believe I'd let it go for so long. I should have come over and just started talking to you." he confessed, taking the last bite of his sandwich and finishing his milkshake.

"I am sorry you thought I was still angry with you because I wasn't. I never even considered that we had so many mutual friends. Jenny told me you weren't invited to parties because everyone thought it would upset me. But I wouldn't have been upset," he reassured me.

"I remember when my dad told me to fix it. I was about thirteen. But I never did. I wanted to, but I didn't know how. I'm truly sorry," he explained.

"What do you mean you didn't know how? Inviting me to your party might have fixed it. But don't worry about it anymore. I have tons of friends. I don't need your friendship or your friends."

"I want to be your friend," he said."

"Why?" I asked, genuinely curious.

"Because I like you and hate myself for screaming at you. I forgot that you sometimes laugh when you are nervous."

"Yes, you mentioned that," I said, pouring us glasses of sweet tea, assuming he would enjoy it as much as I did.

"Thanks," he said, taking a drink, "This is great. So how do you think those men got inside your house?"

"I probably forgot to lock the back door."

"Why don't I check everything for you and ensure it's all locked up," he suggested.

"I'll go with you," I said eagerly, wanting to ensure everything was secure. The lingering presence of those men who broke into my house still unsettled me. As we found a window open, and my belongings were scattered about. "Those men touched my things," I whispered to myself.

Hutch overheard me and looked at me with concern. The frown on his face would scare an Army of intruders.

I swiftly gathered my things and headed to the laundry room, 'I won't wear anything those men touched.' I declared, throwing everything in the garbage. I continued to whisper to myself.

Hutch locked the house up, and then he looked at me. "Are you going to be okay?"

"Yes, I'll be fine. Don't worry about me," I reassured him, attempting to sound brave even though he could see right through my facade. "It's not every day someone breaks into my house. Actually, this is the first time. But I'll be fine."

We walked to the front door, and I had to bite my tongue to avoid asking him to stay with me. Because deep down, I was scared. "I'm not scared," I told myself. *'Beatrice, shut up, for crying out loud!'*

"Beatrice, why don't I stay here tonight?" He suggested. "I can stay in one of the other rooms or on the couch."

Grateful for his offer, I nodded in agreement. "I'm going to get my bag from the truck," he said, walking out the front door.

"I'll go with you," I responded, following him outside and across the street. He retrieved his duffel bag from his truck, and we returned to my house together. "If you don't want to stay, I understand."

"I wouldn't have said I would if I didn't want to stay. Would it be alright if I shower?"

"Of course, make yourself at home. You can pick whatever room you want. Thank you for staying. I'll see you in the morning."

He nodded, and I went to my room. Contemplating what

to do next. *What am I going to do? You're not going to do anything.* "You have to be as normal as you always are, shower and go to bed." I took a shower, put on my warm pajamas, then climbed into bed, clutching the other pillow. I set the alarm for five, ready to face a new day.

I woke up to the sound of the alarm, but my reluctance to get out of bed led me to hit the snooze button repeatedly. I couldn't remember how many times I pushed it, but when Hutch asked me if I planned on getting up or sleeping in, I immediately sprang to my feet. Thankfully, I had put on my long pajamas; I usually wore a little bitty T-shirt to bed.

I must have looked like crap the way he was looking at me. "What time is it?

"It's five-thirty," he said.

"What? Oh my God, I'm going to be late," I said, as panic rushed through me.

"I made some coffee; here, this will help you wake up," Hutch said, offering me a cup.

As I turned to face him, I couldn't help but notice how hot he looked this early in the morning. My hand acted on its own, reaching out to brush his curly hair away from his eyes.

"Why did I do that?" I scolded myself. "He is not yours to touch, Beatrice Rose. Keep your hands to yourself." "Thank you for waking me up and for staying the night. I better get ready. Thank you for the coffee," I said, ignoring my embarrassment.

Hutch cleared his throat before speaking, hesitating for a moment longer. "Sure thing. I better head to my mom's and start painting her kitchen," he said. Although unsure if he would actually leave, he continued to watch me. "Are you going to be alright?"

"Yes, I'm fine. I was scared last night, but I'm fine today," I said, trying to sound strong.

"Okay, I'll be seeing you around," Hutch said, turning to leave. I wasn't sure he would go he was still watching me. Then he nodded and walked away.

I reminded myself firmly that Hutch was my enemy, well, not really an enemy, but he was the one who had initiated the conflict between us. I couldn't allow myself to think of him in any other way; it would only bring me pain. Determined, I entered the bathroom and took a good look at myself.

The reflection staring back revealed a disheveled appearance, I went to bed with my hair wet, and it was all over the place.

"Well, I don't want to impress him anyway," I thought as I dressed, put my hair in a ponytail, and grabbed another cup of coffee on my way out. Double-checking that all the doors were locked, I headed towards the hospital. Along the way, I stopped to grab a McMuffin and hot cocoa.

Upon arriving at the hospital, I exchanged greetings with Linda the lead nurse. "How are you doing this morning?"

"I'm doing wonderful. My Penny had her baby last night. I can't wait to see her. She's a little girl. Oh, she's so sweet. Penny sent me a picture."

"Are you going to go visit with her?"

"Yes, next month we're taking two weeks off. We are going to see Penny and her family. I can't wait to see all of them. I know they move all over with John in the service, but I so want them to move here near us."

"Maybe they will when he gets out of the service."

"I pray that they will. Here is your schedule for today, Doctor. There is a new child here with us today. He was in an accident late last night, and they brought him up this morning. His mama is sleeping in there with him. His daddy is in ICU.

I walked into the new toddler's room first. I checked all of his vitals, and he seemed to be sleeping soundly. I looked at his pregnant mother and whispered. "When is the baby due?"

She replied in hushed tones. "Next month, but I think I'm in labor."

"Lay down here, and I'll check you. Were you checked when they brought you into the hospital?"

"Yes, everything was good, but I've been having sharp pains for the last hour. I'm afraid to leave Charlie by himself. He'll be scared all alone."

I knew when she started having another contraction, and when I examined her, I could see the crown of the baby's head. It was evident that the baby would arrive at any moment. We had to improvise and move her into another space with no available rooms. I called for Linda's assistance, and she understood the gravity of the situation as soon as she saw the distressed mother. I delivered the baby girl in the hallway while Linda supported the mother. "Well, it looks like you get to hold a newborn girl today after all," I remarked while Linda cared for the baby.

"She is beautiful," Linda complimented, addressing the young mother. "Once Doctor Price checks her out, you can hold her. But first, we need to get you cleaned up. I'll call a couple of nurses from the maternity department. Who is your doctor?"

"My doctor is in California. I need to call my parents. We were visiting them. Can you call them for me?" the young mother requested, visibly distressed.

"Stay calm, honey we are here to help you. What is their

phone number?" I let Linda take care of everything while I examined the baby. She was perfect. Suddenly I heard a noise and looked at the mother. "Linda," I put the baby in her arms as I jumped on the bed, trying to help the mother to breathe. "Call code blue. We need help." I shouted. Other nurses came running. We pushed the bed in the elevator and up to surgery.

Aware of what needed to be done, I made a small incision in the mother's throat and inserted a tube handed to me by another nurse. I carefully guided it into the opening, allowing her to breathe properly. Simultaneously, I took a deep breath, relieved that the procedure was successful.

"You did it, Bea." I got off the bed and looked at Cassie.

"We did it, Cassie, all of us. How did you know I would need that tube."

"I saw you running, and I had a whisper in my ear that said, grab a tube."

"I love the way you listen to your instincts," I praised her before explaining the situation to Dr. Patrick McNaught, who had taken over attending to the young mother. Dr. McNaught hadn't changed at all since our school days, persistently asking me out every time we crossed paths, hoping I would eventually say yes. The young mother was rushed into surgery, and I turned around to return to the pediatric floor.

"Good job, Bea. I'll take you to dinner tonight," Dr. McNaught suddenly interjected.

"Can I bring my boyfriend?" I countered.

"You have a boyfriend?" he replied, clearly taken aback.

"Yes."

"What's his name?"

"His name is none of your business."

. . .

"Just as I thought, you don't have a boyfriend. Remember, I've known you since you were three. I know everything about you."

"His name is Hutch," I stated firmly, ending the conversation.

"Hutch, who?"

"Hutch Campbell. Goodbye," I said as I turned on my heel and walked away.

I screamed at myself in my head for saying that out loud, but my mouth wouldn't shut up. It kept right on talking. What is wrong with me? Now everyone would hear that I'm supposedly dating Hutch Campbell. He owes me for what he put me through growing up. What if he has a lady? Then too bad? I am not going to tell Patrick McNaught I was lying."

3

HUTCH

We were going to Florida to assist a family of eight girls who needed to hide from their father. He intended to sell them to the highest bidder—or so he told them. "What kind of father does that?" I asked, appalled. "He must be trying to scare them into marriage."

"Jessie Robinson says he's fed up with his daughters not finding their own husbands, so he's decided to find them a husband himself," Noah explained.

"What's his nationality?" I asked.

"He's from the United States and was born in Florida, as were his daughters. But his family came from Egypt. Their mother says they need to be hidden until their father comes to his senses."

Curious, I inquired further, "Where are we taking these eight young women?"

"We've acquired a bed and breakfast on the Oregon coast. It has plenty of rooms and security cameras already installed. Our job is to pick them up and keep them hidden until their father realizes his mistake," Noah replied.

"I heard a piece of gossip yesterday," Noah said, looking at me.

"If it's about me, I'm sure it's not true," I joked.

"It's about you and a certain doctor," Noah said, looking at me.

Concerned, I warned him, "Don't spread false rumors about Beatrice. I've already put her through enough growing up. I won't tolerate any lies circulating about her. What exactly are they saying?"

"They are saying that you're her boyfriend."

"Why would they say that?"

"Because Bea told Patrick McNaught she couldn't go to dinner with him unless her boyfriend could also go with them. When he asked who her boyfriend was, she said Hutch Campbell."

I couldn't help but laugh at the absurdity of it all. I looked at my buddies. "She's just using me as an excuse to avoid dating guys she's not interested in."

"What if Judith hears about your 'new girlfriend?'"

"So, what if she does? I'm not in a relationship with Judith. I've only gone out with her a few times. I'm a free man, and if Beatrice wants to use me as an excuse, not to date, then I'm happy to oblige," I declared.

"But that also stops you from dating other women, doesn't it?" Noah reminded me. "Or did you forget that?"

"Fuck, I completely forgot about that," I said, realizing the predicament I was in. "Beatrice is really getting back at me for the way I treated her in the past."

As we approached our destination, Ryker announced that we were landing soon. There were five of us total, including Ryker, who would be the pilot on this trip. We laughed when we saw the large bus, we would be driving to pick up the girls. I climbed behind the wheel, and we set off on the hour-long journey to retrieve the sisters.

The drive was scenic along the coastal road. When we arrived, I glanced at my watch. It was seven in the morning. I hoped the sisters were all awake. Because we were picking them up and leaving, as we walked to the front door, it was opened. *Good, everyone looks to be awake and ready to go.*

The girls greeted us eagerly. "It's about time! Let's get out of here before my father shows up. Seriously, I thought you guys were professionals." I watched as eight young women walked past us.

"Don't mind her. Charlotte is the oldest sister and will be the first to be sold off."

I watched as they walked to the bus, each carrying their carry-on. I was relieved they didn't have loads of suitcases.

The ladies took their seats, and we left. "Can we get your names, please, and we'll know who we are talking to."

"My name is Theresa.

"I'm Mandy."

"I'm Rachel

"I'm Kim."

"I'm Mary."

"I'm Ava."

"I'm Joy, and the grumpy one is Charlotte."

"My name is Hutch. These are Noah, Leo, and Jackson. Ryker will be flying the plane. He won't be staying with us. I'm sure you will eventually meet all of us. But for now, four of us will be with you."

"You follow our rules. No phones allowed," I stated firmly as I handed a little box to one of the sisters. "Please put your phones in here and make sure they are all turned off—no computers of any kind. While you are with us, you need to follow our instructions."

One if the sisters protested. "We're not babies. I'm thirty, and the youngest is twenty. You are supposed to keep our father from finding us. You are not our babysitter."

"Do you want your dad to find you?"

"Of course not," she replied.

"Well, then you need to listen to us? Your father can track you through your computer. Once you open that laptop, he'll find you. It's pointless for us to hide you if you don't follow our instructions."

"What are we supposed to do then?" another sister asked.

"We have board games at the safe house. You can play board games. Or take walks. We're in the country, so there are tons of things to do. Think about what people did before computers and phones were invented. They engaged in healthy activities and didn't spend all their time on their phones."

"I know how to enjoy outdoor activities. We all do. But I have a business to run. I have no time to take workdays off and play board games," another sister complained.

"We were hired to protect you until your dad stops acting like an idiot and wants to sell you off to the highest bidder."

"I don't know why he's doing this, and I don't care. I'm just doing my job. I know you have a business to run. But right now, you can't run it. You need to let your assistant take care of that, or whoever. Why is your dad doing this to all of you?" I inquired.

"Because he wants grandkids. We think he's trying to scare us, but he keeps introducing men to us, so we don't know what he is doing. I don't think that I should even have to be in on this. I'm the youngest; Charlotte needs to give him grandkids. If she doesn't want to marry, she doesn't have to. You can get artificially inseminated. Have a child let grandma and grandpa play with it, and let us get on with our lives," the youngest sister explained to her oldest sister, who looked like she wanted to wrap her fingers around her neck and squeeze tightly.

"Yeah, Charlotte, this is all your fault. If you weren't so stubborn, maybe somebody would propose to you," another sister chimed in.

As the girls continued to argue, I couldn't help but wonder about the one who remained silent. Are any of you dating anybody right now?" I asked, attempting to change the subject.

"Mandy was dating someone. Who was that, Mandy?" one of the sisters asked, possibly Mary. *Or was there even a Mary?* I shook my head and listened to the sister's conversation.

"Can you mind your own business, Mary? If I'm dating someone, that's no one's concern but mine and his. Besides, Dad doesn't like him. It wouldn't do me any good to tell him I would get married and have kids. He would disown me, and then he wouldn't be playing with his grandkids," Mandy replied defensively.

"Amanda Mae, look at me," Charlotte interjected. Are you planning to elope or something with Ben? I think it's damn time we tell the others who he is. I know you've been sneaking around. My friends have seen you."

"Ben? You've been dating Ben?" Rachel asked; all the sisters turned their attention to Mandy.

"Oh, for Pete's sake, can I please have some privacy in my life? Why do you think you must know everything about our lives, Charlotte? I don't ask you questions about your life, so you can't ask me questions about mine. And the same goes for you, Rachel." Mandy snapped.

. . .

Observing Charlotte's scrutinizing gaze, I watched as she locked eyes with her sister. "Tell me, what the hell is going on with you?" she demanded.

"Why do you think something is going on with me?"

"Because of the way you're acting. You might not want to tell me right now, but I'll get it out of you," Charlotte replied, determined to uncover the truth.

"I'm sure you will. Now stop staring at me. Lord have mercy, will you ever stop being so nosy in our lives? Just because you're the oldest doesn't mean you get to know everything happening in my life. I'm twenty-eight, for crying out loud."

Despite Mandy's protest, I couldn't help but wonder what she was hiding. Now I want to be nosey. *What is Mandy hiding?* I knew we would eventually find out; we just had to be patient. As we neared the airport, Theresa announced she was starving. Since we hadn't eaten either, we stopped at a drive-through for food.

I wrote down what everybody wanted, I went inside, and ordered our food while the others stayed on the bus with the girls. The aroma of the food filled the air, reminding me of how hungry I was.

It took forty-five minutes before the food was ready, mainly because Charlotte had requested different items that had to be cooked differently. She believed thas how she made sure her food was cooked fresh. So, it took longer for them to cook it. I knew by the time we got to the airplane, Ryker would throw a fit, so we ate our food while driving.

I had a feeling this was going to be a very interesting job. Hopefully, the young ladies wouldn't argue throughout the entire time we were assigned to protect them. I was right. As soon as we got on the plane, Ryker wanted to know where we'd been.

"We stopped and got something to eat. I got you two cheeseburgers and a Pepsi," I said, handing him his hot food.

"Thanks, I'm starving."

Three hours later, we landed in Oregon, where a bus was waiting for us. I took the driver's seat, as I had done with the previous bus. Once everyone was aboard, we headed to the safe house.

The safe house was situated in the forest, it was beautiful, with green trees and flowers meticulously planted everywhere. I thought this would be the perfect place to have a family vacation, which I shared with the girls.

"Think of this as a family vacation, where there are no phones or computers—just the eight of you sisters enjoying each other's company," I suggested.

"I think we'll have a nice time," Joy said, smiling at her sisters. "Look how beautiful it is here. We'll enjoy ourselves. It's no one's fault but our father's. So why don't we forget about what Daddy is trying to do to us and enjoy being with each other?

"Oh, Joy, it's easy for you to say. You're one of the younger girls. Daddy's not going to make you get married first," another sister commented.

"I looked at Charlotte, the oldest. "Do all of you live at home?"

"None of us live at home."

"I'm still unsure how your father thinks he can force you to marry someone. This is the United States. You can't force your children to get married."

"You don't know my father. He's a bully when he wants his way.

"Even our brothers can't save us from this."

"Where are your brothers?"

"One lives in London, and the other is a Green Beret. He's the one who suggested our mother hire you guys."

"Do we know him?"

"His name is Carter Robinson."

"Lieutenant Robinson is your brother?"

"Yes."

"Is your father as good at getting his way as Carter is?"

"No, Carter has a way of speaking to you that you don't know you've agreed with him until it's too late. He's done it to us many times. Our father threatens us with silly things like his death, so we end up giving in. But we can't give in this time because he won't ever give up on us getting married, and having children."

"Exactly. I told you Carter was a smooth talker," Noah said. "Are you ladies like your brother?" Each sister pointed to Mandy.

"I wouldn't be here if I could talk my way around things," Mandy said, frowning at her sisters.

"Your rooms will be on the second floor; I'll leave you to find them yourselves," I said as I walked into another room and tossed my duffle bag onto the bed.

4

BEATRICE

I should never have claimed that Hutch was my boyfriend. I desperately hoped he hadn't overheard what I said. But knowing this town, the news probably spread from one end of our little town to the other. Cedar Falls has a way of spreading the news so fast that even the smallest fib can transform into an elaborate tale.

I sensed trouble brewing when Mrs. Tumble embraced me at the grocery store and exclaimed, "I always knew you two were meant to be. All it took was accepting his apology, and love would flourish."

"What?" I exclaimed, bewildered.

"No need to play pretend with me, dear. I spoke to his mama, who mentioned he spent the night at your house during the burglary incident. My heart is brimming with joy. I can't wait for the wedding and those adorable babies." I bolted out of that store faster than a roadrunner.

What the hell have I done? Damn it. I need to talk to Hutch. But I didn't want to. I prayed he hadn't caught wind of the gossip. I went by his house, but he wasn't there. I stopped at Gilly's and Gray's boatyard.

As I stepped out of my car, Gray paused from sanding the boat and straightened up. Then Gilly and the baby emerged from their beautiful Victorian home. "Are you here to help us with the boat sanding?" Gray asked.

"No, not this time. I was looking for Hutch. I need to talk to him."

"Does this have anything to do with you two dating?" Gilly enquired.

"Yes, it does. I can't believe you already heard about it. I innocently made a passing remark, and suddenly it morphed into a never-ending saga. Good Lord, I was stopped four times at the grocery store. I have to explain what's happening to him."

"He's away on the job right now."

"Dang, do you know when he'll be back?"

"I'm sorry, I have no idea when he'll return. Are you okay?"

"I just really needed to talk to him. But I suppose I'll have to wait. Can I at least hold the baby?"

"What a darling baby. I envy you two. You have a family; what more could a person want?" Gilly put her arm around me. Damn it, I didn't mean to make them feel sorry for me.

"You'll have a family someday."

"I've never been in love before," I admitted, deliberately avoiding mentioning my enormous crush on Hutch.

"Well, if you tell guys who ask you out that you have to bring your boyfriend, you'll never find a man that way," Gray said.

"If you know that much, then you know who it was."

"No, I don't know who it was."

"Patrick McNaught."

"McNaught? I'm sure he's changed. He's a doctor, and

they're nice people. He can't be the same person he was in high school," Gray said, frowning.

"He's exactly the same person he was in third grade. He used to bully me just because he wanted to be friends with Hutch."

"He only wanted to join us in playing sports. We should have let him play." Gray said.

"He wanted more than that. Are you suggesting I should go out with him?" she asked.

"No, I'm saying we should have let him play baseball with us, and maybe that would have made him easier to get along with. I have a good friend I would like to set you up with," Gray said, still frowning.

"No, thank you."

"Your problem is that men are afraid to ask you out because you have something about you that might intimidate them."

"What do I have that would scare men off?"

"Besides being beautiful, you always carry yourself with such confidence, as if daring someone to challenge you," Gray said. "I've known you forever, and that's always been a part of who you are."

"Yes, well, I had to learn that because of Hutch. You know what? To hell with him," I declared, turning towards my car and realizing I was still holding the baby. I looked at Gilly and offered a smile. "I suppose I should leave this little sweetheart with you."

∼

WHY DID everything have to go back to third grade? Would it be better if I relocated to a new town? I loved Cedar Falls, but my entire life seemed intertwined with Hutch and that damned door. Would my life improve if I moved away?

Perhaps I should explore other towns. I would be leaving my patients, but maybe I could continue my practice for a while. I've allowed that incident from third grade to dictate my life for far too long. That night, as I lay in bed, I thought over everything.

When I climbed out of bed, I walked through my house, and then I made my way out back to my beautiful, landscaped yard. I had made up my mind. With a heavy heart, I called my friend Stephanie. Hey, Steph. I want to sell my house."

"What? I thought you loved your house. I heard about the intruders. Are you okay? Is that why you want to move?"

"Yes, I'm fine. It's not about the intruders. It's about Hutch. I do love my house. I'm so tired of everyone waiting to see what will happen between Hutch and me. It's been like this since he returned to town. You know how I feel about Hutch," I explained.

"Is it because of that little white lie you told?" Stephanie inquired.

"Some of it is because this town has always been so concerned about what happens between us. I'm tired of it. I'm tired of seeing him across the street. I'm tired of remembering all the parties they had that I wasn't invited to. Put my house up for sale. I need a new environment."

"I'm getting pissed remembering how I felt as a teenager watching all those kids show up across the street. Of course, most of them would come over to see me and go back and forth," I said, remembering.

"Okay, I'll do it. When do you want to start?"

"I'm leaving for vacation in a month. I'll use that time to

explore other towns where I might want to live. It should be somewhere along the coast, where it's cooler."

"I can't believe that. This is your town as much as it is his. Don't move away," Stephanie urged.

"I don't know what I'm going to do. Put my house up for sale next week. That'll give me time to put things away. I don't want anyone going into any room alone. I don't want them touching my things."

"Alright, sweetie, I'll put it on the market. You do know that's prime property. You'll never find anything like it again. It's the perfect spot for raising a family."

"I know it is. I thought I would be raising my family in that home. But I have to get away from Hutch. Can you imagine my children having to hear stories about their mommy and that man, Hutch who lived across the street? I told you how I felt when he spent the night at my place. I'm losing my mind since he moved back home."

"You are not losing your mind. You're a woman with intense emotions."

"That's easy for you to say. You have a man who loves you and two perfect sweethearts."

"I know I am lucky. Your problem is you work all the time. How about I find you a date?"

"Oh please, I feel like I'm back in high school, and you and Sandra are trying to fix me up. The guys we knew didn't want to anger Hutch by asking me out. Gabe asked me out. I went to dinner with him but left when I sat at the table. He had to bring up that damn door."

"Do you want me to bring the papers over or just list your home in the metro? We won't put a sign up; too many people would start snooping around?"

"Okay, whatever you do, I'm sure it will be perfect. I'll see you after my vacation."

"Where are you going for vacation?"

"I don't know yet. I might visit with my parents for a few days and then start looking at where I will live. The only thing about seeing them is they start in on me about having babies. What is with people these days and babies? Oh, I forgot you are one of them."

"You're their Godmother, so stop it."

I chuckled; I couldn't help it. "I love those little people so much. You know I'm jealous. I'll drop you a key by tomorrow."

"Okay, I'll see you tomorrow. I love you, Bea. I want you to take this week and really give this some thought."

"I will. Love you too."

5

HUTCH

"Wow, you girls can really sing?"

"Thank you, we used to sing for family members every Sunday. We also sang in church with our mom. I miss Mama. Can we call her so she can visit us?"

I shook my head. "It's been a month. Do you think your dad is still trying to force you to get married?"

"I don't know. Does our mom have your phone number?"

"Yes, she has my number, but she hasn't called me yet." I heard a vehicle drive up, and I walked outside. Grayson got out of his truck. "What's up, brother?"

"I came to see if anything is moving forward."

"No, not yet," I sensed he had something else he wanted to say. "Do you have something else to tell me?"

"Bea is selling her house. Mom said there is a stream of people looking at it," Gray said, surprising me.

"What? Why is she selling it? She loves that house. She had it completely remodeled," I looked at Grayson, feeling a sense of panic.

"I think she's moving away," Grayson said uncertainly.

"What the fuck are you talking about? I want her to stay here. I have to talk to her," I said, feeling my world was falling apart around me.

"She's gone on a month-long vacation. But I think you should call Stephanie about Bea's house. Could you buy it? Beatrice came looking for you. She wanted to talk to you because the town, as usual, has decided that the two of you are getting married and ready to have babies," Grayson said, trying to put it in a kinder way than the elders of our town would put it.

"Fuck, can't people stay out of our lives? This has been going on forever," I grumbled. I was feeling frustrated by the town's gossip.

"My guess is she was tired of everyone asking her when she would give her mama a grandbaby," Gray suggested.

"Those old ladies need to mind their own business. Why did she tell Patrick I was her boyfriend?"

"She wanted him to stop asking her out. She must have forgotten he was the biggest gossiper in town. Some people say she's pregnant, and you won't propose to her," Gray said.

"What is wrong with people? Do you think Steph knows where she is?" I asked

"You can ask."

"I will ask her after I buy Beatrice's home. I won't let a stranger move into that house."

"Well, you better get going before someone else buys it. Take my vehicle," Grayson offered.

"Thanks. My first stop will be Stephanie's," I said, realizing the urgency of the situation as I drove, I couldn't help but wonder what would happen if Beatrice and I dated. I couldn't be around her without wanting her. Could I take her to dinner and keep my hands off her? Yeah, I could do that. I was lost in thought.

"This is all my fault. It's crazy that what you say or do as a child can impact your entire life. I don't want Beatrice to leave her home because people keep interfering in her life."

"Yeah, it's a mess. But you can make it right," Gray said reassuringly.

"Two hours later, I pulled into Stephanie's Realtor's office. She must have seen me drive up because she had the door open when I arrived."

"Well, hello, Hutch. What can I do for you?" Stephanie asked.

"I want to buy Beatrice's home. But don't tell her who bought it. Tell her she has six months to move. I think she is making a mistake selling her home. These busybodies in our town should mind their own damn business,"

Stephanie frowned. "What makes you think she's selling her home because of the busybodies? That's not the reason. Bea is selling her home so that she won't have to remember how her life was growing up here. She was treated unfairly because a small child couldn't hold a damn heavy door open.

"I didn't know that was going on," Hutch replied, ashamed of himself.

"Oh, really. You didn't notice Bea was not going to parties. You didn't notice the other kids ignoring her if you were around. So, she has decided to move and is driving around, looking for another town where she can start over."

"That's crazy. You don't start over for those reasons. I caused all of this. I wish I could change it, but I can't. So, the least I can do is buy her home when she realizes she hates herself for selling it, and wants it back."

"Bea is thirty-three, and she wants a family. No one in

our little town, besides Doctor McNaught and a few others, has asked her out since college because of you. Your friends don't want to make you angry," Stephanie revealed.

"That ended a long time ago. Beatrice still has a lot of years before she has to worry about getting married and having children." *I won't mention this to Stephanie, but I didn't want anyone dating Beatrice.* "I don't want a stranger buying her house. Tell her she can still live in it for a year. Don't tell her who bought it. I'll be back tomorrow to do the paperwork. Then I have to get back to work."

"I hope Bea doesn't beg me to tell her who bought it," Stephanie expressed her concern.

"Just make up a name, any name. I've bought lots of property on this coastline; I don't remember mentioning the other people's names. I'll see you tomorrow," I said walking back to the truck,

"Okay, but don't you think she'll know who lives in it," Stephanie asked.

"I'm buying it for Beatrice because I know she loves that house," I stated firmly.

"Your mother told Mrs. Tumble that you stayed at Bea's house all night," Stephanie mentioned.

"What? Why would she say that?"

"Because you did stay there."

"But Beatrice was scared. I told my mother about the intruders. Damn it, this town needs to stay out of everyone's life. I'm going to the next town hall meeting and telling them to mind their own fucking business."

"Why do you care if Bea sells her home? Why do you suddenly care about these old biddies talking about Bea? You've been back in town for a year, and now you notice things. That's bullshit. Spill the beans, Hutch. Do you have feelings for Bea? If anyone spent time with Bea, they would easily fall for her."

"Have you always been a pain in the ass, Stephanie?"

"Only when I'm standing up for my friend. I constantly hate myself for not telling you to stop this when we were in grade school. I hate you for the way you treated Bea."

"Join the fucking crowd. I don't know why I let it go on. I stopped talking to her; I didn't mean for everyone else to stop talking to her. I think I was embarrassed to tell her how sorry I was. Did Beatrice complain about it growing up?"

"Beatrice never complained about anything. You should know that. I think if she was to ever complain about anything, it was how heavy the door was for an eight-year-old girl," Stephanie replied.

"Just stick the knife in further, why don't you? I'll see you tomorrow," I said, feeling guilty and frustrated. *How could one little thing that happened when you were a child hurt someone for all these years?*

"Okay, I'll see you around ten. Will that be good for you?"

"Yes, that's good." I walked back out to the truck. What a mess. I needed to talk to Beatrice to understand what was happening. She shouldn't have to change where she lives because of something that happened when she was eight, which would never have been a big thing if I wasn't acting like a frigging idiot.

I drove over to my mom's house; I got out of the truck as she opened the back door. "Hey, sweetheart, what are you doing here?"

"Gray has taken over for me for the night. Did you know that Beatrice was selling her house?"

"I heard something about it. Why is she selling her house? She loves that house. She's in that yard every weekend planting flowers and digging stuff up. She's always bringing over flowers for me. She gives me bulbs to plant when her garden gets overloaded. Why would she want to move?"

"Mom, do you remember when my hand got slammed in that damn door, and I was so angry at Beatrice," I took a deep breath. "I should have told Beatrice two days later that I was sorry, and I didn't blame her for that door shutting on my hand."

"But I didn't tell her or anyone else. When I came home when Dad had his heart attack, I apologized for my behavior and not talking to her. I'm so sorry for giving her the cold shoulder. Because of me, most of the kids in this town shunned her if I was around. She wouldn't have been invited to parties if I had gone."

"Because of that incident when she was eight years old, she was ostracized by almost every kid I hung around with. We weren't mean to her. We ignored her all the time. We hurt her so much, that poor little girl, I am so angry with myself."

"Now it's something completely different being spread around that we are secretly dating, and Beatrice may be pregnant. When you told Mrs. Tumble that I spent the night at Beatrice's house, Mrs. Tumble saw Beatrice in the grocery store and couldn't stop telling her how happy she was about us being together."

"Oh, dear, what have I done? I had no idea Mrs. Tumble would do that. She must have left out the part about me telling her about the intruders. She made it sound like you guys were having an affair."

"I have to talk to Beatrice and apologize to her, just don't tell Mrs. Tumble anything," I requested.

"I won't be telling her a thing anymore," Mom assured me.

I didn't dare tell Mom about buying Beatrice's home. I won't tell anyone about that. "I'm going to go home to get some rest. I'll see you in a few weeks."

"Okay. Hutch, I'm so sorry about this. I hope we didn't run Bea out of town. Why Beatrice's family is the first settlers in this town," Mom said with sadness.

As I drove home, I saw Mace walking down the street with his daughters and he was carrying the baby on his shoulders while the three girls followed behind. It was so heartwarming to see him happy with Hannah. They were so happy together.

I rolled my window down and greeted them. "Hello," They all shouted hello and waved, even the baby. Then he grabbed his daddy's hair to keep from falling. Mace laughed out loud.

Once I got home, I walked into the kitchen, looked around, and then walked to my room to shower. I've lived in this house for eight months, and it still looked and felt unlived-in. I think that was because I had spent most of my time at my mom's, a block away.

She always asks me to spend the night, knowing she must be lonely. I stayed at her place as much as I could. Jenny and her family moved twenty miles away, so she doesn't have the grandkids as much as she used to. I just hoped she hadn't replaced her loneliness with gossiping with her friends.

I arrived an hour early at Stephanie's office at nine instead of ten, "You're early."

"I have to get back to work,"

"If you trust me to finish filling out the forms, I'll have you put your signature everywhere it goes."

"Of course, I trust you. I need to relieve Gray, or he'll want me to take over for him when I don't want to. If you know where Beatrice is, will you let me know?"

She looked at me like I asked her to spill all her secrets. "No, I won't let you know. Why would you think I would? You and Bea aren't dating. You aren't even close friends. Just because you stayed at her house one night when she was scared doesn't mean crap. Sure, that was nice, but it is the only nice thing you have ever done for Bea, or did you forget that?"

"No, I haven't forgotten anything about Beatrice."

"Good. I'll file these papers and ensure Bea doesn't know who her buyer is," she said, getting up and holding the door open, signaling that our conversation was over.

I took my time driving back to the safe house. When I arrived, the sisters were playing volleyball. Jackson was on one team, and Leo was on the other. I smiled at my brother Gray as I threw him his keys. "Do the ladies know Leo played college volleyball?" I asked.

"I'm sure they don't, but Jackson thinks his team can win anyways. He and Leo used to play volleyball on the beach while attending college in Southern California."

"Thanks for covering for me," I said, changing the subject.

"Were you able to talk to Bea?"

"No, she's out looking for a new town to live in. Remember me telling you about the men who broke into Beatrice's house, and I stayed there that night? Our dear mother told Mrs. Tumble that I stayed the night with Beatrice. Now the old crazy-as-a-bat-ladies are saying she is pregnant."

"Fuck, why the hell would Mom even spread that around? She knew it was because Bea was scared. Did she forget to mention that to Mrs. Hot-Wire-Gossiping Tumble? Lord, what a mess," Gray said, annoyed. "Now you have to marry her?"

Gray laughed it off, but I was thinking the same thing. "Yes, she did forget that part when retelling her story. Beatrice is on vacation for a month. Hopefully, I can speak to her before she buys another house."

"I'll call you if I see her around, but I'm leaving for New York on Wednesday," Gray said as we went our separate ways.

I stopped walking and looked at Gray. "What's going on in New York?"

"Some bigshot needs a few guards. I talked Mace into going, plus Gabe is going."

"Who is it?"

"We don't know. There's a show they are going to see. They also have guests going, so they wanted three guards. Gilly mentioned that she would accompany me to determine if the person they're seeing is important or just another wannabe seeking attention."

"You know Gilly; she's devoted to the shipyard. I've never seen anyone work like she does," I remarked, shaking my head.

Gray smiled and shook his head. "She wants Joe to experience it in all its glory. She believes he's reaching the end of his life because of his age. Gilly wants to recreate the shipyard's past when Joe's family owned the business. However, Joe has repeatedly assured her that it looks better now than ever. She has a very big heart. Plus, she loves the shipyard and Joe."

"Yes, she does. Who would have thought the woman you saved on that oil rig would become your wife and the mother of your child?

"Life always has a way of working out. Some call it fate."

"I've never been one to believe in fate."

"Oh really, I would have thought you, of all people, believed in fate."

"Why would you think that?"

"Don't you think it was fate that had you over at Mom's the night those men broke into Bea's house?" Gray said, with that cocky smile on his face.

"I'd say it was lucky for her that I was there," I chuckled.

"You, do know she could take both of them down."

"Why didn't she?"

"My guess is she didn't want to hurt them."

I started laughing, shaking my head. "I think she has all of you fooled. She asked me to stay all night because she was scared. If she could take them down, she would have done it before I arrived on her doorstep."

"In that case, she must have fooled the entire town. They all thought she could take care of herself. Why would she want the whole town to believe she could care for herself?"

"She won't have to worry about that if I'm around. I will make sure no more bad guys get close to her."

Gray looked at me and shook his head. "That is unless she finds another house in another town before returning."

"Sometimes I think it would have been better if I didn't move back here. Now it feels like everyone's watching to see what will happen next."

"Tell me how you feel about Bea. I have never seen you so concerned about anyone as you are about her."

"What do you mean? I'm always concerned about people. It's just that I don't often come across individuals who need my concern. I was genuinely worried about Gilly and Lucy when they needed me. I never expected Beatrice to become a person I care about, but now I am," I confessed, avoiding eye contact.

Gray looked at me, not saying a word, "Okay, I'll be honest. I want her. Being near her takes my breath away in a good, hotter-than-hell way. Now you know. I've felt like this since high school. If only I had done things differently. We could be married and have children."

"So, do something about it. You still have time to fix everything. Don't overthink it; that's always been your tendency. You have always been that way. Go after what you want. What do you have to lose?" Gray said, staring me down.

"All I know is that it's in our nature to protect women. So, if I'm concerned, it's just a part of who I am."

"Maybe you don't need to be. I'll tell you a little secret that I've noticed since I've been married. Women seem to be more dramatic than men. Sometimes they exaggerate about what really happened. If you tell Gilly I said that, I'd deny it."

I patted him on the back and couldn't hold back the laughter that burst out of me. "Damn, brother, you've been spending too much time around women."

"I only spend time with one woman. Trust me, if you ever get married, you'll notice they enjoy gossiping with you."

I was still laughing as he got into his truck and drove away. I went into the house and took out some steaks for a barbecue. I took out the frozen garlic bread.

"Welcome back," a voice greeted me, and I turned around to see Mandy holding a basketball.

"Are you guys going to play basketball?" I asked.

"If you want to join, I should warn you that we're really good at most games. Growing up, we competed against other women's basketball teams, and most of the time, we always won. "So, just giving you fair warning."

"Oh yeah, well, we played a little basketball in college. So you don't have to worry about winning. It'll be four against eight.

"Yes! Let's do this."

"Let me change my shoes." I walked to my room and changed. When I walked back outside, I stood there in shock as I watched the Harlem Globe Trotters Women's team. I looked at my buddies. "I had no idea we were playing against professionals."

"Okay, let's get this game started," Rachel said, loud enough for everyone to hear.

They murdered us. We knew within the first five minutes of playing they would slaughter us. I have never laughed so hard in my life. Whenever we thought we had them, one of the girls would pop up in front of us, blocking our shot and taking the ball.

"I told you we almost always won," Mandy said, smiling.

"Where did you learn to play like that?" I asked, astonished.

"Our father had all of us playing basketball when we were old enough to , a ball. He had all of us watching the Globe Trotters games. He had all their videos, plus they were friends of his. It is one of the games we've always loved playing," Mandy said, smiling.

"Is your dad a basketball player?"

"He used to be. He always said he thought he would

have enough kids for a basketball game, but he had mostly girls. So, he taught us how to play." I saw her hand go to her stomach and she frowned.

"Are you ok?"

"Yes, just a small pain."

6

BEATRICE

I made the trip to Seattle intending to explore the possibility of moving there, but it didn't take long for my mind to shut that idea down. The city was undeniably beautiful but overcrowded, and it wasn't easy to find a parking spot. None of the towns I visited during my trip appealed to me enough to consider relocating there.

In the end, I realized how much I loved my hometown and didn't want to leave it. I decided to ignore anyone who bothered me, particularly someone named Hutch Campbell. With that decision in my mind, I headed toward home, and called Stephanie to share my news. Selling my home was off the table.

"I've had a change of heart. I don't want to sell my home. I love it too much to leave. I would miss all my friends, even some who aren't my friends."

"So, you are not going to move after all?" she asked.

"No, I'm staying put. I'll be back home in two days. Although I did have a great road trip. But next time I'd prefer some company. None of the towns I visited were as beautiful as our town. I'm just grateful that you didn't sell my house," I said relieved.

"I never even put a sign up in your yard," Stephanie assured me.

"Great, I can't wait to see you. I'll talk to you in a few days."

"Okay, call me when you get home."

"I will."

AT THREE IN the morning my phone kept ringing incessantly. I reached over and grabbed it. "Hello, who is this?"

"It's Hutch, Beatrice," I could hear the worry in his voice.

"What's wrong," I asked, already sensing something serious had happened. I knew Hutch wouldn't have called me unless it was an emergency.

"We need you to come where we're staying. One of the young ladies we're guarding needs a female doctor. She won't see or talk to anyone else. I don't know the severity of the situation because she won't tell me. She's very emotional. I hope it's okay that I called you."

"Where are you?" He asked.

"I'm about a two-hour drive from home. Where are you?" I asked, sitting up and getting out of bed.

"We are outside of Florence, Oregon. Are you anywhere near us? I can have the plane pick you up."

"I'm in Florence, Oregon. Give me your directions," I said, feeling a sense of dread washing over me. I wasn't particularly fond of coming face-to-face with Hutch Campbell. Thirty minutes later, I pulled into the parking lot of a bed and breakfast where Hutch was waiting for me. I grabbed my bag, and he rushed me inside and upstairs.

The room was full of young women. I saw the one lying in bed as the others stood around, wiping their eyes and sniffing. "Whoever isn't the patient, please leave the room," I said in my firm doctor's voice. They all left except one. I looked at her. "My sister needs me with her.

Then I turned my attention to the woman in bed. "I'll be fine, Charlotte. I want some privacy." Though she didn't want to leave, Charlotte eventually nodded and left the room.

"Tell me why you need a doctor?" I asked gently, approaching the bed.

"I am so scared, and I upset my sisters when they saw me crying. I didn't mean to make such a fuss," she replied, gripping her stomach as if in pain. "No one knows this, but I'm pregnant. Before coming here, I took three tests just to be sure, and I'm having horrible cramps as if I had started my period. Please don't let anything happen to my baby. I have to tell my family. Charlotte was right; I do need her."

"How far along do you think you are? Are you experiencing a lot of pain?" I asked, trying to keep her calm.

"I've been here a month, so I'm six months pregnant. The pain isn't unbearable, but the cramps are worrisome. We had a basketball game, and I might have overexerted myself. I don't want any harm to come to my baby," she confided, her anxiety evident.

"I'm going to examine you and see what is going on with the baby. It could be a false contraction; Those are quite common. How long have you been experiencing the pain?" I asked, trying to keep her calm for the exam.

"I woke up at eleven, and my sister Charlotte sleeps in that bed," she said, pointing to the other bed. She was reading. Charlotte loves reading romance books and sometimes she'll read all night long and still go to work, or she used to. We all have our own homes now. I'll have to tell my sisters about this. They won't let me be alone after this."

"Have you ever had an examination from a doctor?" I asked as I began the examination.

"No, this will be my first time," Mandy replied.

"I'm a pediatrician. I know all about babies," I reassured her. Are there any other areas of your body that hurt?"

"My breast feels tender to the touch. I want my mama," she said, tears streaming down her face.

"Can you call her?"

"No, Hutch said we couldn't contact her until this situation was over. If my father knew I was pregnant, we could all go home. But I'm afraid he would tell Ben, and Ben would force me to marry him."

"Do you want to marry Ben?" I asked.

"Yes, but I want him to propose to me without knowing we are having a baby," she replied.

"Does he know where you are?"

"No, nobody knows."

"Perhaps you should let Ben know where you are and see what happens. Right now you need to take it easy. Can you do that? Can I trust you to stay in bed for a few days?"

"Yes, I can do that."

"Would you like to use my phone and make a quick call?" I offered.

"What about Hutch? He'll be angry."

"Don't worry about him. We won't tell him," I assured her, handing her my phone.

As Mandy dialed Ben's number, I stayed with her in the room. "Hello," Ben answered.

"Ben."

. . .

"Baby, where the hell are you? Tell me so I can come and get you. Your crazy father needs to be locked up. I'm going to bring you home. Give me the address," he demanded urgently.

"I can't do that. I just wanted you to know I'm fine. I'll call again when I can," Mandy responded, her voice trembling.

"No, sweetheart, don't hang up. Mandy, I love you. I will always love you. I want you with me forever. Tell me where you are?" Ben pleaded. "I want us to be together forever."

"I'll be home in a couple of days. I'm going to call my mom. Goodbye, Ben. I love you too, she wiped her eyes and looked at me. "Can I call my mother? I need her with me right now."

"Of course, you can," I said.

Mandy hung up the phone, and I looked at her. "Do you want your sisters in here with you? Are you ready to tell them you are having a baby?"

"Yes, I'll tell them. Can you stay with me?"

"Yes, I can. You need some rest. I'll give you something for your cramps and get your sisters," I said. When I opened the door Mandy's sisters were waiting in the hallway. "Your sister wants to talk to you."

They all rushed into the room. Charlotte wiped her eyes. "What is wrong with you."

"Nothing is wrong. I'm going to have a baby," Mandy whispered, but everyone heard her.

"A baby." They whispered in unison. "How far along are you?" Charlotte asked.

"I'm six months pregnant. Ben is the father, and that is why I never said anything. I love him, and he loves me. Mom will be here in the morning. I'll tell her when she arrives," Mandy said.

Joy's eyes widened in astonishment. "Ben Branson, is the father? Oh my Lord, Dad will kill him. What can we do? I'm going to be an aunt." She began crying and hugged Mandy. Don't you worry. We'll stick close to you. We won't let Dad shout at you. Do you love Ben?"

"Yes, I'm in love with him. This wouldn't have happened if Dad weren't so jealous because Ben is building the new resort in Hawaii. Dad wanted that job. Ben has already stepped back so Dad could win the bid for a job he wanted. But he won't do it anymore. I told him he can't keep trying to make friends with Daddy If Ben asks me to marry him, I'm going to say yes. I'm having a baby in three months."

"Is Ben in Hawaii?" Joy asked.

"No, he's been hunting for me. I told him I would see him in a couple of days. But I'll call him back and tell him I need him here with me. When Mom arrives, will all of you please stay by my side?"

"Of course, we will. When did Mom say she would be here?" Charlotte asked.

"Sometime this morning. I'm sure she's on her way. I'm going to go back to sleep. I am exhausted," Mandy replied, visibly drained.

"Can we please write down names?" Joy asked.

"Yes, I'm so happy all of you know about the baby. I was so scared. What a relief it is to share this with my sisters." She put both hands on her tummy. "The baby is moving come and feel her."

"Is it a girl?" Joy asked, her eyes shining with excitement.

"I think so," Mandy replied

I smiled as I watched Joy touch her sister's tummy. Suddenly she made a little noise and jumped back, exclaiming, "The baby in there kicked me!" Laughter and tears filled the room, and I had to wipe the tears from my own eyes.

"I'll leave you to visit for ten minutes, and then you can go back to sleep."

"Thank you so much, Doctor Price."

"You're welcome. Remember, just ten minutes. Mandy needs to stay on bed rest for a few days. So, if you all decide to leave, please ensure Mandy stays off her feet for a while. What happened was the baby letting you know it's time to rest," I explained, smiling to ease any lingering anxiety.

"You listen to the doctor Mandy. We won't let her get out of bed," Ava said reassuringly with a comforting tone.

"Ava, I need to get out of bed to use the bathroom and shower. The doctor doesn't mean I can't do those two things," Mandy giggled, lightening the mood.

As I made my way downstairs, I discovered Hutch in the kitchen, busy cooking. Noah, Jackson, and Leo sat at the table, drinking coffee. "How is she?" Jackson asked. Hutch poured me a cup of coffee.

"She's six months pregnant. Their mother will be here later. Mandy's father doesn't like the man she loves, who is also the father of her baby," I explained.

"All he wanted was a grandchild, and now he's going to get what he wants. Here you go," Hutch said, placing a plate of delicious-looking pancakes on the table before me.

"These are delicious. My favorite pancakes are chocolate chip. Can I have two more, please? What is this place?"

Jackson pushed the syrup closer to me before answering. "It's a safe house, we bring people we're guarding here, and other places."

"It's truly a beautiful place. Aren't you all going to eat?" I inquired, noticing they hadn't served themselves.

"We've already eaten. What a miracle that you happened to be so close," Leo said. "Is she going to be alright?"

Mandy is fine. I believe her anxiety was making her sick. She had this big secret inside of her, unable to share this beautiful news with anyone. Now she can put her life together with the man she loves," I replied, observing Hutch's watchful gaze. He placed two more pancakes on my plate, diverting my attention.

I loved food, and everyone I knew enjoyed feeding me. That's why I run every morning with Cassie. That way I can eat what I want.

Hutch pulled a chair out and straddled it; he was so close. "Can you stay for a couple of days?" he asked, his proximity making me slightly uncomfortable.

Clearing my throat, I responded, "Umm, yeah, I promised Mandy I would be here when she told her mother. I wouldn't be surprised me if her boyfriend appears behind her mom, maybe even before her mom."

Jackson looked at Hutch. "Do you think that'll cause a problem?"

"We'll have to wait and see. I hear the others coming down to breakfast."

Hutch remarked, returning to the cooking. I offered my assistance, but he seemed preoccupied. I noticed he was making blueberry pancakes instead of chocolate chip. You're making blueberry pancakes and not chocolate chip."

"They prefer blueberry," he muttered under his breath. The sisters were excited about the baby and their mother's arrival.

Ava spoke up, addressing her sisters around the table. "We should start packing now that Daddy will have his grandchild he'll leave us alone," She took two pancakes, "These are delicious. Thank you, Hutch."

. . .

"You're welcome. Let's get this straight. Are you telling me all of you get to go home?"

"Well, we intend to go home unless this upsets my father further because the baby's father is his enemy, or so he believes. But he's not our enemy. Daddy and Ben are top architects who always compete against each other. Ben has tried time after time to get along with my dad. I didn't know he was Mandy's boyfriend," Ava explained.

"Mandy doesn't want Ben to know about the baby just yet. She wants him to marry her because he loves her, not because she's pregnant," Joy continued, sharing more intimate details.

"Joy, you don't have to tell Hutch everything, Charlotte interjected."

"I just want him not to say anything if Ben shows up," Joy replied, voicing her concern.

"Do you think Ben is going to show up? And who gave your mother this address?" Hutch asked as he turned and looked straight at me.

Charlotte shook her head. "I don't know. I guess Mandy did."

"Beatrice, were you in there when she called her mother? Oh, wait. Of course, you were she used your phone. Did you ignore me when I said no phones? What if she was hiding from a deranged husband, and he showed up with a gun?"

"I know you would not let anyone get hurt," I assured him.

"How do you know?" he challenged me.

"Because I've known you since I was two. You've lived across the street from me forever. You might be an ass most of the time, but when those intruders broke into my house, you ran in and saved me," I spoke as Gabe, and Noah started laughing. We have all known each other forever.

"What's so damn funny?" Hutch asked, staring at the guys.

"Are we not allowed to laugh?" Jackson said, with a huge grin on his face.

"I'm being serious. We don't know who will be coming here with their mother. It could be some crazy guy angry because the woman he loves has been hiding for over a month."

"Okay, I'm sorry for laughing. I know you're serious," Jackson turned and looked at me. Did you talk to their mother?"

"No. Mandy's mother doesn't know about the baby yet. Mandy will tell her when she arrives in a couple of hours. Mandy is still asleep. Once she wakes up, I'll get her something to eat. Unfortunately, I can only stay until tomorrow. I have to go back to work on Monday," I explained, aware of Hutch's disapproving frown.

"What? I wanted you to stay until the sisters leave," Hutch expressed his disappointment.

"Why?" I asked, genuinely curious.

"They need you," Hutch replied, his frown melting away as a hint of a smile played on his lips. Despite his serious demeanor, there was an undeniable attraction about him.

I smiled to myself, thinking even when Hutch was frowning, he was still hotter than any man I've ever known. Then I asked the sisters if they needed me to stay. They reassured me they would be fine and would most likely return to their homes once Mandy told their mother about the baby.

However, they did enjoy talking to me. I thanked them for their kindness and then mentioned that I was feeling exhausted and wondered if there was a place I could rest. Hutch offered to show me to a bedroom. I followed him down the hall. As soon as I saw the large, comfortable bed, I crawled into it without uttering a word and quickly succumbed to sleep.

7

HUTCH

As soon as Beatrice's head hit the pillow, she drifted off to sleep, clutching my blankets and hugging my pillow. I stood there, drawn to her, very tempted to crawl into bed beside her. What was happening to me? This was Beatrice Price, the same Beatrice I had ignored all those years ago. I my had blown my chances with her twenty-five years ago by acting like a big child. My heart hurt when I thought about Beatrice.

Shaking off those thoughts, I left the room and made my way to the kitchen. It was my day for kitchen duty, so I began tackling the stack of dishes piled up in the sink. Three hours later, Beatrice emerged onto the front porch just as a car pulled into the driveway.

"That must be the girl's mother. Thank you for letting me borrow your bed," Beatrice said as I joined her on the porch.

"You're welcome. You can borrow it anytime you want," I replied, a hint of something more in my tone.

"Thank you." *Did Hutch Campbell just come on to me?*

"How did you know it was my bed?" I asked, genuinely curious.

"It smelled like you," she replied with a smile.

I couldn't help but smile to myself. Beatrice Price knew my scent. We walked down as the taxi driver opened the car door for the girl's mother.

"Hello, Mrs. Robinson."

"Please call me Gwen," she replied warmly. She was elegant and beautiful. No wonder the girls were so beautiful. This woman was... that's when I recognized her, Gwen Harley, she was a famous top model.

"Okay, Gwen, this is Beatrice Price. She's the doctor who came to see why Mandy was sick."

"What is wrong with her? I've been so scared, Gwen said."

"Nothing that time won't heal. Why don't we talk to Mandy? There is nothing for you to worry about," I reassured her.

"Mama, I've missed you so much!" Ava said, running up to hug her mother. Then the others came running, and Charlotte took her mother's hand. "Let's go see Mandy." I followed behind them as they walked up the stairs.

"Why does Mandy need me?" Gwen asked Charlotte. Confusion was evident in her voice.

"We're here. Now you can talk to Mandy," Charlotte replied. Leading them into the room. Gwen's eyes met Mandy, who was sitting up, and eating a bowl of ice cream. We gathered around the bed as Gwen embraced her daughter.

"Sweetheart, how are you?" Gwen asked, her voice filled with concern.

"Mama, I'm going to have a baby," Mandy revealed.

I stood in the hallway, waiting to see how everything turned out.

"Oh my, a baby! A baby! Gwen exclaimed with excitement. I'm going to be a grandmother," she said excitedly, "I'm so happy. Have you told Ben?"

Mandy's eyes widened. "How did you know about Ben?"

"I saw the two of you having dinner. I'm so happy for you. Ben is a good man. I'm glad he's the father of your child. How many months until the baby arrives?"

"Three more months. Ben is on his way here. He'll be here anytime. I know Daddy isn't going to like me being with Ben, but we love each other," Mandy explained.

"We have three months to do a lot. Your father respects Ben; he'll be happy that his grandchild has Ben for a daddy. Of course, you'll have to get married," Gwen suggested, her mind already racing with plans.

"Mama, I don't want to tell Ben about the baby just yet. I want him to want to marry me because he loves me, not because I'm pregnant," Mandy said, her voice filled with tears.

I motioned the man into the room where the women were, and I stayed out in the hall listening to everything they had to say.

"Sweetheart, I love you more than anything in this world. I will always love you. I've loved you before our baby was conceived," he sat beside her and pulled her into his arms. "Sweetheart, will you marry me?"

"Ben, I'm so happy you are here. Yes, I'll marry you." We all watched as he pulled her into his arms and kissed her.

"Tell me why you are in bed."

"I just needed some rest from overdoing things."

"Do we get to go home now?" Ava asked.

Gwen turned to Ava. "Well, your father is getting his grandchild, so I say yes, we can all go home."

I heard the entire conversation from the hallway, waiting for my chance to speak. I heard Beatrice talking.

"I'm going to leave. I think you have everything taken care of. I have to get back to work on Monday. If any of you are in Cedar Falls, Oregon, please stop by and visit me."

"Bea, thank you for coming to check on me."

"I'm happy to have met all of you," I heard Beatrice say. "You all must realize how lucky you are to have each other. I want to have a large family like yours if I ever get married. Mandy, I want a picture of that baby."

"I'll send you one, I promise. Bea, I'm sure you will get married. You are so beautiful inside and out."

"Thank you," Beatrice said softly before saying goodbye and turning to leave.

She's leaving. My heart was pounding in my chest. I didn't want her to go, but I knew I couldn't stop her. I couldn't help but imagine myself being the father of all those kids.

When Beatrice noticed me leaning against the wall, she stopped. "So, you're leaving us?" I asked, trying to hide the longing in my voice.

"Yes, I need to get home," she replied, her voice tinged with a hint of disappointment.

"Why don't you leave in the morning? You can get a fresh start," I suggested, my heart pounding with nervousness.

"Why would you want me to leave in the morning? I'm sorry, I forgot you don't hate me anymore. Even though staying another night sounds tempting, I must get home," she explained, her voice trailing off.

"Would it be alright if I take you to dinner when I get

back home?" I blurted out, feeling a mixture of anticipation and anxiety.

Beatrice looked at me with disbelief in her eyes. "For some reason, I'm unsure if that's a good idea. I mean, do you even like me?" she asked, her voice barely above a whisper.

"I've always liked you," I confessed, my heart racing. "I just didn't know how to talk to you without looking like an idiot. When I didn't talk to you, I wanted to. It's just I didn't know how to start. I knew you hated me, and I'm ashamed of myself for the way I behaved. I've carried that shame for so many years."

"Hutch, don't be ashamed of yourself. That's crazy. I want you to forget everything about me from when we were growing up," she urged, her voice filled with compassion.

"But will you forget it?" I asked, overcome with regret and longing.

"Is dinner out of the question? I inquired. "I mean, if we had grown up together, we might be married by now, on our way to having a bunch of kids."

"You say the most outrageous things, Hutch. Goodbye," she retorted, walking away from me."

"I'll see you around, Beatrice." I stayed where I was for a while longer. I heard someone and turned my head. Ava stood there. "You have to keep trying. Never give up," she advised.

"I won't," I replied, my determination renewed.

"We are going to be leaving, I hope the bus is ready for us," Ava said, watching me closely. "I'm going to miss you guys."

8

HUTCH

"I can't believe you want me to leave again. I just got home," I protested.

"Would you rather I left? My wife has just told me she's pregnant. I want to celebrate with her," Gray replied with a grin.

"Oh, I bet you do," I smirked and couldn't help but chuckle. "Do you realize how scorching hot the desert is right now? It's one hundred and twenty degrees; I just checked. I will burn up in that damn desert," I continued to argue. Even though I knew I was going.

"It's not like you'll be walking across the desert. You'll be under the air conditioner most of the time. You won't even know it's hot outside," he said, trying to reassure me.

"Alright, I'll go. Congratulations on the baby," I said, happy for my brother.

"Thanks, brother. I knew I could count on you. I'm taking Gilly out for dinner tonight. Cassie is our babysitter for the night," Gray said, trying to change the subject. He just remembered that Hutch wanted to be the babysitter.

"When are you going to let me be the babysitter?"

"I didn't know you wanted to babysit," he lied. "When you get back, you can babysit for us. I'm sure Gilly will make you stay at Mom's while you babysit."

"That breaks my heart. I'm trustworthy, and you know it."

"Hutch, I'm kidding. Of course, you can babysit. I'll tell Gilly myself."

"So, do I still have to go to the desert?"

"Yep, sorry."

"I'm going to run by Mom's. I'll see you when I get back."

As I pulled into Mom's driveway, Beatrice was there. It had been a month since I last saw her, and my heart started racing. When she saw me, she got up to leave but changed her mind. She sat back down. I caught a glimpse of the smile on my mom's face, hoping she wouldn't immediately call her friend to gossip about it.

"Hey, Beatrice, how have you been?" I greeted her, hoping she couldn't hear my heart beating from where she sat.

"I'm good. How about you?" she replied.

I hugged my mom and took the empty chair. "I'm leaving for the desert in thirty minutes. It's a hundred and twenty degrees there now, and I'm not looking forward to that kind of heat."

Beatrice watched my every move, clearly wanting to say something. "I received a letter from Mandy. She's getting married and has invited me to the wedding. She said she's also invited you and the guys since we had a big part in their getting together. I wrote back to her and said it was all her doing. They were in love, and that's why they're together. So, what's happening in the desert? Or is it top secret?"

I caught myself daydreaming, listening to her voice. For

some reason, I always thought she was one of those women sitting quietly in a chair with little to say. I smiled to myself; I'm so damn happy she's not the quiet type. Then I remembered she was waiting for me to say something.

"No, it's not top secret. I'm helping search for a runaway child. I can't imagine how a child could endure that heat. He's fourteen years old," I noticed how alert Beatrice became.

"What made him run away?" Beatrice inquired.

"What?" I responded, momentarily confused.

"How old is the child?"

"He's fourteen."

"Right, you already told us he was fourteen. Why do they think he ran away?"

"His stepfather said he was angry about something and ran off. The stepfather went looking for him when he didn't return within two hours. A team of people is searching for him right now. I'm not sure why he was angry, but I'll get to the bottom of this."

"Where was the mother?"

"She wasn't there. The boy and his stepdad were spending the weekend together. The mother said her husband had planned a surprise getaway just for the two of them."

Beatrice shook her head. "Richard, is that the boy's name?"

"Yes."

"The stepdad is lying. There's no way that boy would willingly go away with his stepfather. Their relationship isn't good. Why would he choose the desert in the middle of summer? We need to find out where he's hiding that boy. I'm going to grab a bag and go with you."

I sat there, stunned, watching her dash across the street. I glanced at my mom. "Did she say she was going with me?"

"Yes, she did," my mom confirmed.

"Don't tell anyone that Beatrice is joining me. I don't want any gossip going around about her."

"I won't utter a word," my mom assured me. I could tell she was contemplating who she could trust to share this information with. "I understand, dear. I won't breathe a word."

"Mom, I'm serious. You can't tell anyone."

Beatrice returned, "Did you bring hiking boots? I brought extra cool towels for us. I guess we should get going. I packed some food and sweet tea; I'm sure you're starving."

"Yes, I suppose we should. I need to swing by the house and get my bag. Bye, Mom."

"Goodbye, you two. I pray you'll find that boy alive."

I was still in disbelief that Beatrice was going with me. My insides were jumping up and down with joy.

"I should have asked if I could come along, but all I could think about was that poor little boy in the scorching desert hiding from his stepfather," Beatrice admitted.

"Did you watch that movie on Netflix about that crazy stepfather?" I asked her.

"Yes, it was a horrifying movie," she replied.

"Exactly. So, you can understand why I felt compelled to help when Gray told me about this boy. Since we watched the same movie, we'll plan our approach together. Where do you think the boy is?"

"It depends on who owns the place in the desert. If it belongs to his mother, he might know a place to hide because he has explored the property before. If it belongs to his stepfather, then there is no telling where he's hiding. I hope he's hiding and the stepfather hasn't harmed the boy," she said, shaking her head.

"That's what I was thinking. We need to find out who owns the property. Hey, I think we make a great pair of detectives. I don't know what Gray will say about you going with me, but I want you to know that I will not let anything happen to you.

Beatrice smiled and reached over and patted my hand. "I know you won't. Are we friends again?"

"I hope so," I said, looking down at my hand with hers still on it.

"Then we are. I'm glad I have you in my life again. Just think I'll be able to visit with our friends without rushing to leave because I see you there."

"I'm so sorry about everything."

"Don't worry about it. It wasn't that bad. Most of the time, I was with all of my friends, and they wouldn't let me leave a party. It was even fun sometimes when we would always try and hide from you."

"Good."

9

BEATRICE

I sat on the private plane, still amazed at myself for impulsively telling Hutch I was going with him. I should have asked first, but I didn't want to risk him saying no. I chuckled out loud, remembering the look on his face when I announced I was going. His mother is probably already on the phone with Gray and won't be able to keep it a secret, so she'll call her friends. But I was determined to find that boy, and if I got to spend time with Hutch, all the better.

"Are you not working this week?" Hutch asked, smiling at me.

"What?" I asked, turning to look at him, feeling a little embarrassed that I had been caught staring.

"I asked if you were off this week?"

My eyes widen in shock. How could I forget I had to go to work? I took out my phone and called Kathy, my receptionist. "Kathy, you'll have to reschedule my patients. I won't be in this week."

"Not at all."

"No, not at all. I'm sorry I wasn't able to call earlier. This just came up, and I'll be out of town."

"Okay, but you have to spill the beans when you get home. My Aunt Trudy called and told me you'd be out of town with a hottie. You can't even imagine how surprised I was."

"What? I'm on a mission to save a child. Nothing more."

"If you say so Bea, I believe you," she giggled.

I hung up the phone and looked at Hutch, "That's the problem with hiring one of my best friends. She forgets I'm her boss," I knew my face was red, but there was nothing I could do about it.

"I swear my mom is one of the nosiest people in town now. She must have called everyone. The older women decided to play matchmaker for us. We'll ignore all of them."

"We will?"

"Are you upset about Kathy's Aunt Trudy?"

"No, I'm a little surprised she found out so soon, but I don't mind. This gives them a reason to call each other. I've lived across the street from your mom my entire life and knew she couldn't keep a secret for long. She always calls and tells me what's happening in town."

"Does she? She calls me too. I did tell her not to gossip."

"If I could get through us sneaking around and me being pregnant, I could get through this." I almost moved out of town because of the pregnancy before I came to my senses. I saw the laughter in his eyes, and we burst out laughing.

"Since Jenny moved out of town, Mom has been lonely, so I guess she gossips now."

"Hey, whatever it takes to keep her strong. Loneliness is very unhealthy. People who live alone and never see others don't live as long as someone with people living with them."

"I didn't know that. I visit her as often as I can. Now with Gilly being pregnant, maybe she'll see them more often."

"I didn't know about Gilly being pregnant. She's so lucky." I shook away the sadness, but Hutch looked at me strangely.

"Why do you say it like that? I'm sure you'll have a house full of kids one day. How many bedrooms do you have?"

"Five."

"You can always add on. You have a large property or make it a two-story."

I burst out laughing. "How many kids do you think I want?"

"I know how many you want. You want a dozen kids. When you were around six, you told me you didn't have kids to play with because you were an only child. I said when you get married, you can have a bunch of kids, and you said, 'I want to have a dozen,' and then you asked me how many was a dozen."

My eyes turned all watery as I remembered that conversation. This was the first time someone had ever reminisced about that childhood dream, and it meant the world to me that he remembered it too.

"Why are you crying?"

"I'M NOT CRYING," I said, turning my head so he couldn't see. He touched my face, turning it so I was looking at him.

"What would you call these?" he said, wiping my tears with his thumb.

"Those are silly tears. I just realized that you're the first person who's ever remembered something about me from when I was little. Plus, I remembered that silly conversation,"

As the plane was landing, Gabe interrupted us. "Hutch, we're landing, and Bea, buckle up your seatbelts."

"I think Gabe was more shocked to see me with you than you were when I said I was going," I said, chuckling.

Hutch grinned. "I thought his eyes would pop out of their sockets. We should shock Gabe when he lands and walks back here," Hutch said, grinning.

We landed in Death Valley, where the heat was so intense that nothing moved outside. Looking out the window, I saw the heat waves coming off the tarmac. "Where would a fourteen-year-old go when hiding for his life?" He asked.

"I don't know," I replied. "But we'll find Richard. I feel it in my bones."

"What does that feel like?" He asked.

"Hopefulness," I said, smiling.

"I'm glad you feel it," Hutch said.

"Me too," we both whispered, our anticipation building as the plane taxied towards the gate. Gabe made his way back to where we were, and as he approached, Hutch gently turned me around to face him. With a tender intensity, he leaned in, capturing my lips in a passionate kiss. Time seemed to stand still in that moment as I melted into his embrace, my arms wrapped around him, feeling the heat and desire between us.

Caught up in the sheer intensity of the moment, I forgot about everything else except the sensation of his lips on mine. The unmistakable hardness pressing against me heightened my awareness of our shared longing. It resonated deep within me, touching the very core of my being. A fleeting thought of self-doubt crossed my mind, labeling myself as pathetic for giving in to these overwhelming emotions.

"I guess my mom was right. You two are together," Gabe said, interrupting us.

Hutch stiffened, remembering we weren't alone. He rested his forehead against mine until our breathing and heartbeats calmed down. "I didn't know that was going to happen," he whispered against my lips before kissing me again.

I didn't know if I could walk. My body felt like jelly. Hutch put his arm around me and guided me to the door, which was opened. The heat outside hit me hard, and I almost lost my balance.

"Gabe, I'll call you when we find the boy," Hutch said, breaking the silence as we stepped outside.

"As much as I hate to say this, I'm staying to help look for him. We'll have a rental waiting for us," Gabe said,

As we walked to the rental car, Hutch was carrying both of our bags, and Gabe continued to discuss how we would find the teenager. Hutch looked at Gabe and said, "I'm glad we'll have you helping to find him." Worry and concern marked Gabe's face as he voiced his thoughts. "We need to find that boy before the heat becomes unbearable. What possessed the stepfather to bring him to the desert in the middle of summer?"

My mind was still reeling from the unexpected kiss Hutch gave me moments ago. I tried to shake it off and focus on the situation at hand. "Did you watch that Netflix movie last week about the stepfather? I asked Gabe to get my mind on something besides that kiss.

I have been kissed before I even had a steady boyfriend for two years, so I've done more than kiss, but nothing prepared me for Hutch.

"I hate to admit to watching Netflix, but I did see it. Isn't it strange that it was on last week and now this?" Gabe replied, looking at me.

"Exactly what we thought," I said, looking at Hutch. He was watching me, and I felt a tingle in my stomach. "Isn't that right, Hutch?" I asked. I had to pinch his side to get a reaction out of him. And I got a grin instead. All he had to do was lower his head to mine, and I found myself kissing him.

What am I doing?

10

HUTCH

As we drove towards our destination, the heat of the desert was relentless. I wondered why anyone would want to live in such a place. I could see the heat waves coming off the road. We had been on the road for a while when we saw an old truck flashing its lights, and two people were waving their hands at us on the side of the road.

"They want us to stop," Beatrice said from the passenger seat up front. "Gabe, pull over."

"They could be killers who want to steal our vehicle, and it's too damn hot to stop, Gabe said."

"Gabe, pull over," I insisted, seeing Beatrice was getting upset. I had a sense of urgency.

"My girlfriend is in labor, and my truck keeps breaking down. Please help us," the young man pleaded.

Before I could say anything, Beatrice was out of the vehicle running to the old truck, while the young man ran back to his truck. I got out, *fuck* it was hot. I heard Beatrice telling the guy what to do, and then they were transported to our vehicle.

"This is Jim and Patty. They need a ride to the hospital."

"Let's go before our tires melt onto the road," Gabe said, tapping the steering wheel.

I took the front seat since Beatrice got in the back with the young couple.

"They've heard about this missing teenager. Jim, tell them what you told me," Beatrice prompted.

"We both know Richard, and he knows how dangerous the desert is. He grew up here with us. He told me he didn't trust the man his mom married. Richard has been checking him out online. I was helping them hunt for him when Patty went into labor," Jim explained.

"Where do you think he'll go?" I asked, trying to get more details.

"There are a lot of places he would go. But Richard didn't run away, he would have come to one of us. His grandma lives here, and he would have run to her house first. Richard said this guy lied about everything. He wants Jillian's money, but it's Richard's money. Richard's father left everything to him, so first, the stepdad has to kill Richard and then Jillian. Richard tried talking to his mom, but she became angry."

"Is Jillian from around here?" Beatrice asked,

"No, Paco grew up here. He is Indian, and he married Jillian when they were in college. He died three years ago in a motorcycle accident. Richard was very close to his father," Patty said before suddenly crying out.

"How much further to the Hospital," Beatrice asked worriedly.

"Three more miles," Patty panted.

"Gabe, step on it, or this baby will be born in this backseat."

"Jim, you go with them to find Richard. I'll be fine at the

hospital. We need to find Richard. His father was my uncle. Richard is my cousin. I think what Richard said about this man is true. My cousin does not lie," Patty said, in case we would dare say he was a liar.

SHE CRIED out as we pulled into the hospital emergency area; I didn't turn my head. The girl was lying on the backseat, half on her boyfriend's lap, with Beatrice at the other end. People ran out to the vehicle with a bed, and when they opened the back door, we all heard a baby's cry.

"You have a beautiful baby boy, Jim, come around here and put Patty on the bed," Beatrice looked at me. "I'll clean up and be right back."

Patty and Jim were crying. We were parked under the shade when three women ran out and started cleaning the backseat. "Thank you for bringing Patty and Jim. Patty is my sister, and Jim is related to these women," one of the women said.

"I hope you find Richard. Please don't take him to that man his mother married. Poor Richard, our grandma will keep him with her from now on. She always wanted him, but his mother insisted he go with her. Grandma said when we find Richard, he will stay with her here on our land. She will not let him live with a killer. Paco would hate to see his son being hurt by such a man."

Gabe chuckled, still not having said a word, and then he couldn't hold it in a moment longer. "It's almost like everyone is related around here," Gabe said, looking in his rearview mirror.

"We have a lot of family members here, but most of them have moved to Humboldt County in Northern California. They enjoy the cool air. We might move there also. Here comes Jim and the lady doctor. Congratulations, Jim, on your baby boy. Find Richard and bring him to Holly's place."

"Did Holly say that was okay?"

"Yes, she said he can stay with her until the killer is discovered. Grandma is there waiting for Richard. Do you still have everything Richard sent you?" The woman asked.

"Yes, I'll give the papers to these men," Jim said before climbing into the backseat, and we left. When we arrived at the house, the police were there, with the dogs. We got out, and Jim introduced us. "These are the men Grandma hired."

"We didn't know who hired us. So, it was your grandma. She must be pretty worried."

Jim nodded. "Yes, she fears he has already killed Richard."

I watched as the police officers nodded. "What do you guys think?" One of the police officers asked.

"I think Richard is in hiding. I don't believe he'll come forward until the man is gone or someone has proof that what Richard told his mom is true," I said.

"Why don't we go to my place? I have some papers for you," Jim suggested.

One of the police officers stepped in front of Jim. "Jimmy, if you know something, then you should tell us."

"I told you three months ago what Richard told me. You laughed it off. So, I'm sorry I have nothing to say to you."

"Richard is my cousin," I heard a snicker and looked at Gabe. He had his back turned to us. "I will do anything to help him, and you know that," the police officer said.

Jim was shaking his head. "The only thing I know is what Richard told both of us."

"What are the papers?" asked one of the police officers.

"Why don't we let these men take care of everything? Grandma hired them," Jim whispered.

The police officer looked at Jim. "What? Did you say Grandma hired these men? I thought it was Richard's mother who hired them."

"Grandma called his mother and told her about these men. They are former Navy Seals. Now they have SEAL Security. These are the men who will find Richard before his stepdad does," Jim said in a low whisper. Don't let him know that we think he's a killer," Jim explained.

"You are the one who thinks he's a killer. Not everyone else does. Jim, congratulations on your baby boy. Why don't you let us find Richard, and you can stay with Patty at the hospital," he suggested.

Jim looked at the police man shaking his head. "I'm going to help these men as much as I can. Did you know it was Doctor Beatrice here who delivered the baby? I'll have years to be with my baby, and I want to make sure Richard has a long life so he can have his own sons.

"I want to question the stepdad before we leave," I said, looking at the police officer. "Is he inside?"

"Yes, I'll take you inside."

"Have you run his prints? Just to make sure everything Jim says isn't true. It's better to know who we are working with," I inquired as I took Beatrice's hand and followed him inside the house.

"No, but I will," the officer said.

"Don't let him know you are checking his prints. Get his glass when he sits it down or some of his hair," I whispered as we continued to walk into the house. The temperature difference was like we floated to heaven. Jim introduced us to Mick, the stepdad, and I could by looking at him he was just like Richard thought he was.

I don't usually judge people upon first meeting them, but this guy was a loser. Why wasn't he out there hunting for the boy if he was worried about him? I hoped this didn't mean the boy was dead.

"I want you to know we will find Richard and bring him back...." That's when a woman came in crying and shouting. "Where is my son? You bastard, Richard was right. You killed him. Arrest this man. He has harmed my son; I don't know if he killed him; if he did, I will kill him. Tell us where he is, damn you. My baby is in this heat, and we can reach him before he dies. Where is he?" She screamed and attacked the man.

"She is distraught, Jellie baby. You just need to calm down, and then you will realize you're not making any sense," Mick said.

"Not making any sense, you bastard. I did what Richard asked me to do. I had your prints checked out I hired someone to investigate you. You have lied about everything. Mick Strong isn't even your name. It's Jeremy Scott, and we know you have stolen money from eight different women. You're wanted in six States," Jellian shouted before she slugged him in the face.

He tried running, but I grabbed the back of his neck. He turned around and swung his fist. I hit him once, and he was down. Jillian walked over and kicked him.

"We have to find my son. Do you believe this bastard killed him? I don't know what to do."

She was crying, and then she began to shake. Beatrice walked over put her arm around the distraught mother, and walked her to the sofa. The police were reading Mick his rights, but I knew I couldn't let them take him in yet. He was the only one who knew where Richard was.

Beatrice got the woman some water while I looked over

at Gabe. "We need to take him with us. He is the only one who knows where Richard might be."

Jim nodded.

Gabe and I followed Jim to where the police put Mick in the car. I knew it was hotter than hell in that car, so I shut the door to make it even hotter.

"You know if he dies from heat exposure, they'll charge us with murder," the policeman said with a frown as his hand went to his gun.

"What are you going to do, shoot me? He's the only one who knows where Richard is. Let us have him for a while."

"I might as well shoot myself as to let you guys have him," he stopped and took deep breaths. "I'll go with you to ensure he comes back alive."

Gabe got in our rental car and turned the air conditioner on for us. "I need to tell Beatrice what our plans are."

"She's going to want to come with us," Gabe argued. "Dude, you don't know her; I do. She will want to go," he said again, shaking his head.

"She won't want to go. Beatrice knows how hot it is. She isn't crazy."

"We'll see," Gabe said, getting behind the wheel. I heard a noise and turned my head as Beatrice came out of the house carrying a box of things she put in the back of the SUV. She saw me watching her and smiled.

"Is he going with us?" she asked, looking at Mick sitting in the back seat.

"Yes, he's the only one who knows where Richard is. Why don't you stay here with Jillian?"

"No. I came to find Richard, and that is what I'm going to do."

"It might not be pretty."

"I have seen everything. Don't worry about me. Will he tell you anything?"

"I don't know. I might have to beat it out of him."

"We'll do what we have to do. If yours don't work out, I have a few tricks up my sleeve."

"Oh, yeah. I can't wait to see what your tricks are. You sit in the front with Gabe. I'll sit in the middle row with Mick." Since the vehicle had three rows of seats, Jim and the policeman, Richard's cousin, were in the back seat. Mick had cuffs on, so I didn't worry about him trying anything while his hands were behind him.

"Are you going to tell us where you left Richard," I asked.

"I don't know where he is."

"That is not the answer we want. Tell us where he is, or we will drive you fifty miles into the desert and leave you."

Beatrice looked at me as I stopped talking and turned my attention to her as she started talking. "We've been at this for over an hour. I didn't want to do this, but he leaves us no choice,"

"What are you going to do? I hope it's not what I think it is," I said, concerned.

"Hold his head back. I'll do one eye at a time," Beatrice replied, her voice steady.

Not fully comprehending her plan, I played along. "Someone hold his eyes open, and I'll put the acid in one and then the other."

We swiftly grabbed hold Mick's head, and Gabe pulled the vehicle over to the side of the road. "I don't want any of that acid to splash on me," Gabe said as he stepped out of the car. "I also don't want to hear him screaming when the acid starts eating his eye."

Uncertain of what was in Beatrice's little container but realizing it was potent, I watched as she carefully dropped a drop of liquid into Mick's eye. His piercing scream filled the air. "Okay, stop! Hurry, clean my eye! I'll tell you where he is!" Mick screamed uncontrollably.

"Tell us now, or I will do the other eye," Beatrice said, in a low, commanding voice. Mick's desperate plea continued. "He's behind the old warehouse they were going to tear down. It's not that far from here."

As we sped down the freeway, I observed Beatrice squirting the same liquid into her mouth. "What is that?" I asked curiously.

"Fresh squeezed lemons. I always carry some with me. I squirt the juice into my water." Beatrice replied casually.

Finally, Jim spotted the warehouse. "There it is!" h exclaimed as we turned off the road.

"Is he dead?" I asked, turning to look at Mick.

"I thought he was when I dropped him here. Hell, I may as well tell you everything. You already know everything about me. If the kid would have kept his mouth shut, this wouldn't have happened." Mick admitted.

When the car came to a stop, we all got out. Jim began calling desperately, as if unaware that we had just been informed of his death. I pushed Mick forward as we walked behind the building, hoping to find some answers. However, to our surprise, nothing was there—just an empty space. All the doors were locked, making it impossible to enter There was nothing behind the building. We all started calling his name. Frustrated, I got into our vehicle and rammed it into the door, forcing it opened. It was empty of people. We did see some snakes and scorpions.

"Hey, over here are footprints! I called out. We wandered around for thirty minutes when we heard something—a faint sound of singing.

Someone is singing, Beatrice exclaimed, her eyes scanning the area. Then she spotted a spot that went under the building. "Richard, are you in there?"

"Yes, who are you?"

"Richard," Jim shouted. Before he scrambled under the building. "Dude, you aren't going to believe this, but that fucker my mom married tried to kill me. He left me for dead. We have to warn my mom. That fucked up monster said he was going to kill both of us. I wish she believed me."

"She does believe you. She had him checked out." They were still talking as Jim helped Richard out from under the building.

"Let me see where you're injured," Beatrice said, helping the boy to our vehicle. When he saw Mick in the police vehicle, he screamed. "Don't worry about him," Beatrice said, "he's going to prison if he lasts that long." I watched Beatrice wipe her tears, we all wiped our eyes as we watched the boy talking to his friend, who had his arm around him.

"I was just startled for a moment. I'm not scared of him. My arm hurts. He hit me with a bat. He hit my head, and I need to call my mom. Beatrice took her phone from her pocket and handed it to him. She looked at me, and I saw the tears on her cheek. She wiped them away, but the flow didn't stop. She turned away, crying.

"I know I'm an emotional wreck. I'm just so happy he's alive," Beatrice confessed, her voice quivering. Without thinking, I embraced her, holding her as she cried. Uncertain of how to comfort her, I wrapped my arms around her, wondering if it was too soon to confess my love for her.

11

BEATRICE

I can't believe I threw myself at Hutch like that. It's like I exposed my feelings for him in the sand and wrote. "I LOVE HUTCH CAMPBELL." I pulled away and glanced at him, apologizing, "I'm sorry, you must think I'm a water spout. I guess we better get Richard to his mother; I'm sure she is anxious to see him."

Hutch reassured me. "I don't think you are a water spout. This is an emotional time, not knowing what we would find. What about Richard? Do you think he needs to go to the hospital first?"

"No, he can see his mom first, and she can have him checked out. He says he's staying here where his family lives. What a tough decision his mom will have to make—live in Death Valley or lose your son. That's going to be a hard one. Perhaps she should consider that Richard will be going to college in four years, so she should stay here with him until then."

"Her home is amazing, and she has everything she needs there. She has a pool and an outdoor garden that is kept cool. It would be like living anywhere else until you step outside and find yourself in the desert. Everything she has belongs to her son. Her husband didn't leave her anything. She told me she gets an allowance once a month until she remarries."

"What would you do if your husband did that?"

"I would never let myself get into that situation. I have my own money. I would never depend on someone else to support me. I've been working since I was sixteen. I saved all my money for my first car."

"I'm sorry I missed all that. I should have known all about you," Hutch admitted.

"It wasn't exciting, so you didn't miss anything."

"I remember seeing you out front washing your car. I wanted to go over and help you, but I didn't have the right to have you as my friend."

"Hutch, can we forget everything from our past? I want us to be friends without worrying if one of us is angry with the other. I'm not mad at you, and I'm happy we are now friends."

"Me too; I'm happy that we are friends. Are you going to dinner with me when we get home?"

"I WOULD LOVE to go out to dinner with you. Why don't you come to dinner at my house? I'm a pretty good cook."

"What about the biggest gossiper in town seeing me enter your house."

"I don't mind if you don't."

"I don't mind."

I had a huge grin on my face. "Great, how about Wednesday?"

Hutch smiled. "Wednesday sounds perfect."

"If you two are finished planning your date, we can head

back to Richard's house," Gabe interrupted, staring at us. "You two lived across the street from each other for years and are just now getting to know each other."

"We are not going to dwell on the past. The future is all that matters. So, Gabe and all the rest of you former SEALs, keep your opinions to yourself," I declared.

"I guess she told you," Hutch said, and we burst into laughter. The tension eased as we drove Richard home. This case was closed, and the boy was safe. The stepdad would be locked up for a long time, even though they were never officially married.

When we pulled into the driveway, Richard's mom rushed to the vehicle before it had even stopped opening the door and embraced her son. Richard hugged her tightly, and we followed them inside. Richard recounted what happened, and we listened intently.

"He said he was going to kill you next. He thought I was dead. I forced myself not to breathe. As soon as he left, I crawled to a place where I could find shade. There was a water spout under the building, and I saw a couple of creatures under there with me, but I ignored them, and they ignored me."

"Thank the Lord that you are alive. That bastard will pay for what he's done. I wonder if he has ever killed someone. I'll have people looking for everything about this man. I'll make sure everyone he's ever met is at his trial. I can't thank you enough for finding my son. You're welcome to stay here as long as you want to.

"We'll be leaving; I'm happy this turned out how it did. Goodbye, Richard. Jim, thanks for all your help.

Jim smiled and shook my hand. "I'm glad I was here to help you. If you need me for anything, all you have to do is call."

"Thanks, I'll remember that."

I stood there until we had said all of our goodbyes. Then went inside to grab my bag. My mind was consumed with the dinner I had invited Hutch to. What had possessed me to suggest dinner at my place? I must have been crazy not to just go to dinner with him. Oh no, not Beatrice Price; I have to speak up in a moment of craziness and invite him to dinner at my home. He probably thinks I want to jump his bones, which I do! My mind spun with anxiety.

You know he thinks you want him. What have I done? My mind wouldn't shut up as usual. As we drove to the airport, I sat in the back seat, while Hutch took the wheel. It was a peaceful silence until Gabe opened his mouth.

"What are you cooking for dinner on Wednesday? I thought you could cook that stuff you made for the fireman's dinner last year. It was delicious. Or that delightful meat you made for tacos. That's it; you can make tacos on Wednesday, and every Wednesday can be your taco Wednesday."

"Why, thank you, Gabe. Maybe you want to help me cook it," Hutch chuckled, listening to us.

"Maybe I will," Gabe laughed. "Someone has to direct the two of you on a date. When a man asks you out for dinner on your first date, you don't offer to cook for him. You go out a few times to ensure you can trust the guy. Then maybe you can invite him to your place."

The laughter burst out of me, and tears rolled down my face. Hutch joined in, and between laughs he said, "We've known each other our entire lives."

"Do you really know each other? Hell, Hutch, I know more about Bea than you do. You can't jump in with your eyes closed. The least you can do is get to know each other," Gabe advised.

"Gabe, what do you think we are doing? We're having dinner. Now please let Beatrice and me handle our own lives. Beatrice, would you like to get an ice cream when we get home?"

"I'd love that. But I need to shower first. Where are we going for our ice cream?"

"There is a place near where Gray lives. It has the creamiest ice cream. I've been craving it, which is why I usually run there and back home. But you and I will ride in a vehicle tonight, Hutch explained."

"So, would this be our first date?" I asked, smiling because Gabe wiggled his eyebrows at me.

"Yes, I'm thrilled that you listened to me. This is a going-out date," Gabe replied. "So, today is Thursday, and you can go somewhere every night until Wednesday."

"I don't think that's a good idea. If we went out every night, won't Hutch get tired of me?" I voiced my concern.

Hutch butted in. "I will never get tired of you. I have years to catch up on everything I want to know about you. I want to go out with you every night."

To say I was surprised would be putting it mildly. "You do?"

"Yes, sweetheart, I do. If I weren't driving, I would show you how much I want to be with you."

"You would?"

Gabe butted in once again. "Bea, I know you are not used to hearing nice things from Hutch, but you don't have to repeat everything he says."

"I'm sorry, Hutch. Can we drop Gabe off somewhere in this hot desert?"

"I'm sure we can find a spot. I'll slow down, and you can push him out." I asked, giggling at the look on Gabe's face.

Gabe protested. "What? You two wouldn't be talking right now if it weren't for me."

Hutch corrected him. "It wasn't you, Gabe. It was the men who broke into Beatrice's house. We wouldn't be talking right now if I hadn't gone over there. I knew we would talk soon. Every time I saw you, I knew I would go over to your house and beg you to forgive me." Hutch looked at me, "I wanted to talk to you, Beatrice.

"You did? I didn't know that." I admitted, surprised. I'm learning things about Hutch that I never knew before. I didn't know that he watched me while I washed my car or worked in the yard. I always thought he just ignored everything I did or said. Now I know he felt the same as I did. Well, almost the same. I'm sure he doesn't love me, but we can go out on lots of dates. Didn't he say he wanted to go out every night with me?

Gabe continued. "The town will be buzzing like crazy when they see you guys out having dinner and going to get ice cream. It won't only be your Mama talking, Hutch. It will be everyone's Mama talking. Our town will be so excited. You two won't be able go anywhere without whispers following you."

"I don't care," I replied, looking at Gabe and Hutch in the front seat. "If people have nothing better to do than talk about Hutch and me, then let them talk. Their life must be pretty dull if that's all they have to occupy their minds."

During the plane ride home, Hutch and I talked nonstop. It was as if a dam had burst, and everything poured out. We talked about when we were in college. Hutch told me all about when he was in the Navy Seals. We talked about me becoming a doctor.

"I was so proud of you when you became a doctor, Beatrice. I wanted to go to your house and tell you, but I didn't want to upset you. Everybody brags about you being their child's doctor. I'm so proud of you."

"Thank you, Hutch. I wouldn't have been upset. I wanted to tell you how proud I was when you became a Seal. When Jenny told me you were joining the Navy SEAL for a moment, I was so scared I didn't want you going into all those dangerous places. Isn't that strange? We haven't talked to you since I was eight, and it scared me thinking about you going overseas and being a Navy SEAL," I confessed.

Talking to Hutch brought me a sense of peace. I always knew I was going to stay in Cedar Falls. "I love my town. I would never move anywhere else. I thought about moving. I drove all over, looking at other towns, but nothing was like my hometown."

"The old women in our town might be nosey, but that's because they know us. They've known us since we took our first steps. If I moved to another town, nobody would know me, and people wouldn't call out my name and tell me hello when I walked down the sidewalk. You would just be another face in the crowd walking down the street. Isn't that unbelievable that I even went searching?"

Hutch held my hand, gently running his thumb across the top. I wondered if he was going to kiss me, or was that just my desire wanting him to kiss me? "I'm glad you didn't move to another town," he said. If you had, I would have followed you. I sat by the window so I could see you working in your garden or washing your car." To me, your house means Beatrice Price is home. No matter how long I was overseas, when I came home, I would watch your house just to catch a glimpse of you. I couldn't wait to visit so that I could see you."

"I swear, Hutch, sometimes your words make me want to cry. Have you always been like this?"

"Like what?"

"The way you speak. Your words have such an impact on me." Without thinking, I kissed him—right on the lips. I didn't even finish my sentence. "Can we say this is our third date?" I whispered, lips lingering against his.

"Yes," he said, pulling me closer and returning the kiss. My hands found their way under his shirt, caressing his back. Then I realized where I was and hastily retreated to my side of the seat, taking a deep breath. "I'm sorry. I shouldn't have started that. I just couldn't help myself."

"I couldn't help myself either, Beatrice. We'll do this right. I won't risk losing you again. We belong together. I know we're moving fast, so we'll slow down. I want you, Beatrice. I want you so much I know I can't touch you, or I'll lose control."

"I want you to lose control, Hutch. Let's wait until we get home, and then we can both lose it," I replied.

"Are you sure we're not moving too fast?" he asked, his voice filled with concern.

"Time is slipping away. I'm turning thirty-four on my birthday. I don't want us to worry about moving too slowly or too quickly. I follow my heart's lead. I don't always listen to my mind anymore, and I want you as much as you want me."

"I wish you wouldn't say words like that to me while we descend thousands of feet in an airplane, and Gabe is fifteen feet from us." Hutch said.

"Coming in for a landing, everybody buckle up," Gabe announced.

I couldn't help but let out a giggle..

"Why don't we go to the restaurant when we leave here? And then we'll get our ice cream. That is two dates. I say this plane ride is also a date. And then we'll go back to your place unless you want to go to my place, where my mom won't see us," Hutch suggested, watching me.

"No, we'll go to my house. I don't care if your mom sees us. We're grown-ups, after all." I replied.

12

HUTCH

I was incredibly nervous, feeling like it was my first date. Glancing at Beatrice, I still couldn't believe my luck. I wanted to ensure everything was perfect, so I planned to drop her off at home, go home and shower and then pick her up for dinner. "If anyone rings your doorbell, don't answer it." I advised.

"What if someone sees you dropping me off?" she asked.

"You could say you didn't hear them while you were showering."

"Okay, I swear I feel like I'm in high school sneaking around." When we pulled up in front of my home, I looked at Hutch. When will you pick me up?"

"I'll be back in forty-five minutes. I promise."

"Okay, I'll see you in forty-five minutes. Drive carefully."

"Sweetheart, I live around the block."

"I know, but still be careful." I wanted to pull her into my arms for everyone to see. I stepped out of the truck, opened her door, helped her out of my vehicle, and kissed her. I wrapped my arms around her and held her close. My forehead touched hers. "I will see you in thirty minutes."

"Okay," she said, attempting to hide her tears.

"Are you crying?"

"No, of course not. So, it's thirty minutes instead of forty-five?"

"Yes, thirty minutes."

I saw her blinking her eyes fast. I knew she was upset because I saw her tears. I took her bag from the back seat, kissed her again, and walked her to the door. "If the doorbell rings, ignore it. I'm starving, and I want to take you out." I watched as she nodded her head.

After showering in record time, I was back. Beatrice opened the door before I reached it. "Hurry, your mom has been here twice already." She took my arm, and we walked back to my truck.

"You look beautiful. I've wanted to tell you that for the last ten years. You always look beautiful, even washing the car wearing those hot shorts."

"I wish you had told me. I could have started kissing you sooner. Is it okay if I say that out loud?"

"I wish I would have too. Can we make up for lost time?"

"You don't have to do that. Let's focus on moving forward. "Beatrice said. I see your mom looking out her kitchen window. Are we going to keep standing here?"

"Damn, I forgot for a moment where we were," I muttered, seeing my mom walking out of the front door as we pulled away. I put my brakes on. I couldn't run from my mom—the woman who raised me and cared for me through thick and thin. I pulled over and met her in the middle of the yard, and then Beatrice stood next to me.

"Where are you two off to?" my mom asked.

"We're going out for dinner," I replied, hugging my mom.

"You're in luck. I just took a large roast out of the oven.

It's going to get cold tonight," she said, inviting us inside, where it was warm and cozy.

"It smells delicious. Thank you for inviting me to dinner," Beatrice said. My mom couldn't hold back her tears. "You've made me so happy that you two are talking again. It was hard when Bea didn't come to the parties. I'm just glad it's all behind us now. Your father always said the two of you would one day be together," he was right as always.

"We're happy too," I said, taking Beatrice's hand. My mom smiled. I wanted the entire world to know I could finally say Beatrice Price was with me, possibly forever.

"Let's get this food on the table. It gets lonesome in this big house all by myself. I'm so happy to have company for dinner."

"Have you thought about selling it and getting something smaller?" Beatrice suggested.

"I love my house. I don't want to leave. I always thought I would be here forever."

"Have you thought about renting out your bedrooms? You could be like the golden girls from T.V. Maybe some other women feel lonely since they're alone too,"

"I have given it some thought. Maybe I'll ask a couple of people. Now I'm getting excited about it. Now tell me about that boy. Was it his stepfather?" my Mom asked as we all settled down for a cozy family dinner.

"Yes, the man wanted all the money. He planned to kill Richard and then Richard's mother. He believed he had succeeded in killing Richard, but he was mistaken. Fortunately, we were able to locate Richard. As it turned out, he had married seven women before and had swindled them all. But of course, he wasn't married to any of them, only to the first one." After dessert at my mom's house, which consisted of ice cream, we left and headed toward Beatrice's front door. Holding my hand, she guided me inside her house.

"Do you think we're rushing into this?" I asked cautiously.

"What do you mean by rush? We are on our fifth date. This isn't rushing. This is wanting. And I want you, Hutch Campbell."

I reached down and pulled her tee shirt over her head, and then mine ended up on the floor somewhere. I didn't move. I waited for Beatrice to make the next move. It seemed as if any worry about the consequences of our actions flew from her thoughts. At that moment, there was only room for me.

SHE LOCKED eyes with me and pulled me toward her. We found ourselves naked in her bed before she could fully comprehend what was happening. No words were exchanged between us. She pulled me closer and kissed me passionately. I could feel her hands trembling as they ran down my back. "This is all I want," she whispered in a feather-light breath that fanned across my ear. We made love for hours before both of us, exhausted, fell asleep.

I sensed her gaze on me as I woke up. I could tell from her breathing, that she had been observing me. As her hand glided down my chest, I gently grabbed her wrist. Before she could react, I pulled her on top of me, wrapping my arms around her and rolling her onto her back. With my knee nudging her legs apart, I positioned myself between her thighs, supporting myself on my elbows as I gazed into her flushed face. *I love her. I've always loved her. Even though it sounds crazy. Perhaps I'm crazy*

Her heart raced beneath my touch as she lay still,

eagerly awaiting what I would do next. She pleaded in a barely audible whisper, "Don't stop making love to me."

"I will never stop," I replied my voice barely above a whisper. She wrapped her arms around me, providing all the encouragement I needed.

My mouth met hers in a warm and gentle kiss, but it wasn't enough. The taste of her sweet lips left me craving for more. My tongue explored her mouth leisurely until that, too, became insufficient. Deepening the kiss, I tightened my hold on her. With a groan, I raised my head and whispered into her ear. "Tell me what you want."

"I want all of you," she breathed. The eagerness and intensity I felt made it seem like my first time. Although I knew how to please a woman. This was Beatrice. The desire to be with her overwhelmed me like never before. Beatrice was bold and uninhibited, her touch roaming over my back, shoulders, and arms.

Her heart pounded as I caressed her breast, causing her to arch against me and release a soft moan. Restless, her legs moved against mine, I kissed her neck and gradually descended, taking my time to tease and torment her. My tongue playfully traced her collarbone, and when it reached her breast, I felt her tensing beneath me. Slowly, I drove her to the brink of madness. I never realized how sensitive her breast was.

I was losing control my breath shuddering as I kissed her passionately. My hands trembled with anticipation. I kissed her again—hard, quick, with urgency only to pull away briefly to reach for another condom.

She rolled onto her back; her eyes locked on mine. My hands moved to her waist as I pulled her closer to me. I positioned myself between her thighs, feeling a rush of desire as I stretched out. The sensation of her body made me forget to breathe.

My hands caressed her back, the touch feather-light, before I leaned in to kiss her once more. Her touch grew frantic, and she clutched my shoulders, pleading for me to stop tormenting her.

"Hutch," she gasped, her voice a mix of shouting and sighing. My hands had moved between her thighs, driving her to the edge of ecstasy. I knew exactly where to touch, how much pressure to exert. She writhed in my arms, begging me to take her.

Desperation coursed through me, longing to feel every inch of her, to be consumed by her warmth. Her breathing grew more labored, further igniting my excitement. I knew she wanted me to finish and end and torment.

I held back delaying as long as I could to ensure she experienced as much pleasure as she had given me. Her response made it impossible to wait any longer. I knew she was ready. My mouth claimed hers, as I moved between her thighs and slowly sank into her liquid heat. Relishing in the incredible heat and tightness. A groan of pure bliss escaped me as I remained still inside her, panting as I whispered her name.

She cried out my name as overwhelming ecstasy washed over us. Each time we made love felt like the very first time.

"Ah, Beatrice baby," I managed to utter between gasps for breath. Beatrice wasn't content to let me recover. I knew she craved release. She lifted her knees to take me in deeper wrapping her legs around my waist.

She wanted to please me and drive me to the same bliss she experienced. She bit my shoulder, kissed my mouth, and trailed her lips to my neck. Her breath came in pants, heightening the intensity of the moment. I pulled back and thrust deeply, tears welling in her eyes. The overwhelming feelings inside me left me staggered. My movements grew more powerful, more all-consuming, and demanding.

In the midst of raw passion, I had always maintained control, setting the pace. But in that moment, I couldn't control anything. I thrust into her again and again, powerless to slow down.

She was as passionate as me—tension built within her, ready to burst with the need for release. Wave after wave of sensation crashed over her, I thought she might cry.

I kissed her deeply, burying my face in the crook of her neck, taking my time to recover. "Damn, sweetheart, you are killing me," I whispered. I was panting against her ear. Or was that her panting?

Neither Beatrice nor I wanted to let go of each other. Not ever. Wait, what am I thinking?

I rolled to my side, pulling her close. I held her gently, tenderly stroking her. We didn't speak, both content for the moment. Minutes ticked by, and she fell asleep in my arms.

In the middle of the night, she awoke. Her hand reaching out for me, touching me, but I didn't let her know I was awake. She soon drifted back to sleep. When she woke up again, I was in the shower. I watched her through the mirror as she threw her legs over the side of the bed and joined me. I smiled as I pulled her to me and made love to her again. I kissed every inch of her. We stayed in the shower until the water turned cold. You surprise me woman. You are as wild as I am."

"Why does that surprise you? Just because I have an old fashion name from the thirties doesn't mean I'm old-fashioned."

I laughed because I remember telling her she had an old woman's name, when we were little.

"Are you hungry?" I asked.

"Are you going to make breakfast?"

"Yes."

"Then I'm starving."

I reached for her; my voice was a rough whisper against her skin. "Beatrice."

"Yes."

"You are perfect."

"So are you." We both burst into laughter. "I wonder what your mom will say when she sees your truck in the same place it was last night."

"Does that worry you?"

"No, I just don't want her getting on to you, for spending the night with me," she said, smiling. We both dressed and went into the kitchen. I started making eggs and bacon. "That smells so good. I guess making love makes me hungry."

"Then you'll have to run every morning because we will always make love."

She walked up behind me and put her arms around me, and leaned her head against my back. "I'm so happy we talk to each other. I'm sorry I didn't accept your apologies when you tried talking to me. It's because I was so scared, I would screw it up again."

I turned her around and held her in my arms. "Sweetheart, I was the one who was scared of hurting you. I remember shouting at you, and tears fell from your eyes. I knew I had to shut up so you wouldn't cry anymore. I guess I forgot to start talking after that."

13

BEATRICE

"Bea, when are you going to stop running? I can't keep up with you," Gilly exclaimed, gasping for breath.

I looked over at Gilly. "What are you talking about? We've only run three miles."

"I know, but I'm pregnant and can't run as much."

"Who told you that lie? Let me guess, Doctor Gray?" I questioned, raising an eyebrow.

"Yes, he thinks I'll hurt the baby."

"Is he a doctor?"

"No."

"I swear Hutch has been cooking me so much food. If I don't run, I'll get fat. I've already put on a few pounds."

"That's the stupidest thing I've heard. You look beautiful. You have a new glow about you," Gilly said.

"I once mentioned that having sex makes me hungry, and Hutch hasn't stopped cooking." Every time we make love, he cooks," I looked at Gilly, waiting for her to say something. She burst into laughter, so contagious that she had to sit on the beach.

I couldn't hold it in a minute longer. We sat there laughing for at least twenty minutes on the beach. Every time Gilly tried to speak, she would dissolve into laughter. "So, the two of you have been busy. Mom told Gray she's seen Hutch's truck at your place almost every night for the last three weeks."

"Oh, God, I wish there weren't so many busybodies in this town. As my mama always says, if they gossip about me, they aren't talking about someone else."

"Does it bother you?"

"I knew this was going to happen. Hutch said he would walk to my house, but we're adults and don't have to sneak around. I love him. I've loved him for most of my life. I won't let gossip tear us apart. Please don't tell anyone that I said I love Hutch."

"Okay, I won't say a word."

"He doesn't know it yet. He is supposed to be back in town today. They went to rescue some more people out of Afghanistan. It scares me every time he goes over there and some of the other places they go to rescue people."

"I won't say a word, I promise. I'm going home. I have to pee."

"Okay, I'm going to stop by the bank. I'll see you when you bring the baby in for his shots tomorrow."

When I walked inside the bank, I saw Sandy Strand. We went to school together, and here she was with her two adorable daughters. Both girls ran up to me for a hug, and then I embraced Sandy. We have always been close.

"You look energetic and beautiful today. Where did you get those fabulous leggings and that top? I love this outfit. Were you hoping to run into Hutch today?" Sandy asked, grinning.

"No, he is out of town. I was actually running today. I

love these new leggings. They are from Kate Hudson. They are so comfortable."

"I just ordered a double stroller from Amazon that can hold two kids. It's arriving tomorrow. I can't wait to start running with the girls. I doubt if I ever look as good as you do. But I'll look up Kate Hudson's leggings online and get myself a pair."

"You'll love them," I replied, and you have way more curves than I do." I jumped slightly at a noise that sounded like a gunshot. I took the girl's hands and pulled them behind the teller's stand. Stay right there, do not move. I grabbed Sandy's arm and pushed her to where the girls were. "Stay down. Don't get up."

"Bea, get down here with us."

"He has already seen me. Stay down," I whispered."

"Hey, you with the hot clothes on. Come over here where I can keep an eye on you. Stay five feet from me. It would be best if you didn't think you could trick me. I remember you from school. Don't you recognize me? My name is Larry Mathers, and I remember you were good at martial arts. So don't get any closer. Who were you talking to?"

"I wasn't talking to anyone. Yes, I remember you. I thought you moved away from here. You were in my science class. Why are you doing this? Surely going to prison won't be worth how much money you get. Why don't you walk out before someone gets injured?"

"I'm not going anywhere without some money. I want you to shut the fuck up. You were hanging out with that woman hiding with those girls down there. You thought I didn't notice. I saw the two of you talking when I looked through the window to see how many ass-holes were in here."

"Why don't you let the people in here leave?"

"Shut the fuck up." I nodded and took a deep breath, trying to calm myself. I looked around to see who else was in the bank. There weren't a lot of people. I prayed Sandy and the girls would stay down even if he knew they were here. It was safer for them to remain where they were.

I noticed how shaky the teller was. Brenda was expecting her baby in two months. The bank manager stayed at his desk. He was at least seventy-five. I only saw two more tellers. Everyone was scared. I could hear Sandy trying to get the girls to stop crying.

I prayed no one else came into the bank. This guy was so high on drugs he was starting to lose it. "Fill the fucking bags up before I start shooting, he shouted at Brenda. Do you hear me? Do I have to shoot someone to prove how serious I am?" Before any of us knew what was happening, he shot Brenda.

I screamed when I saw her fall, but I was too far away to see her. I looked at the drug addict. "You shot a pregnant woman, you stupid fucker. I'm a doctor, so I'm going to check on her."

"I didn't tell you to help her. You do what I say you do. Okay, you can check on her. I didn't know she was pregnant. I'm not a monster."

I climbed over the counter because I didn't want to bring attention to Sandy and the girls. Once I could turn Brenda over, I saw she was shot in the shoulder. It didn't look life-threatening. I put my fingers to my lips for her not to talk. Brenda watched me as tears ran down her face and into her neck.

"She has to go to the hospital right away. Let her leave."

"I don't need this stress right now," he screamed so loud it scared me, and I cried out when he reached over the counter, and his fist came straight at my face. I jumped to the side. "She can stay where she is. Now you put the money in my bag," He shouted.

I looked around for the money. "There is no money here. That's why Brenda couldn't fill up your bag." I saw someone looking into the bank. It was Hutch's mom. Oh God, please keep her out of the bank. I knew she saw the man with the gun. Then she put her hands over her face when she saw me. She turned and ran to the other side of the street.

Five minutes later, we heard the sirens. I looked at the drug addict. "Now, what are you going to do?"

"Well, Beatrice Price, it's your lucky day. You will be my hostage. I won't get shot if you're in front of me. Get back over on this side of the counter. You will do everything I tell you to do. If you don't, I will kill those little girls down there. Do you understand what I am saying?"

"What did you do before you became a drug addict?" *'Why did you say that out loud, Beatrice?'*

"I'll tell you what I did. I was a husband and a father. I had this wonderful job and was happy until someone broke into my home and killed my family. I had nothing to live for after that. So, you see, I don't care if I die."

"I care if I die. I don't want anyone to die. Just leave."

"You talk too much." He pointed the gun at me, and I saw in his eyes he was going to shoot. I saw movement and turned my head as Hutch ran inside with his gun pointed at the man. I knew it was too late. I should have kept quiet. Now and then, I would hear Hutch; I tried to open my eyes, then I would fade away. He was begging me to live, I wanted to say I will, but I couldn't talk.

14

HUTCH

When Mom's panicked voice pierced through the phone, my heart sank. We had just returned to town, and I was heading straight to Beatrice's house. But then she told me Beatrice was in the bank with the gunman. Ethan overheard her words, and those six minutes that followed felt like the longest in history.

I leaped out and sprinted toward the bank as Ethan's car screeched to a halt at the intersection. My heart was pounding in my chest. With my gun drawn, I burst into the bank. All I saw was the weapon aimed at Beatrice in the gunman's hand. Our eyes locked for a fleeting moment before I pulled the trigger. The sound of the gunshot echoed through the bank as I shot him at the same time, his bullet hit the woman I love.

I saw her fall and was on the floor beside her in less than a second. I had to be careful with her, not wanting to worsen her condition. I located where the bullet went in; it was right behind her ear.

Never before had I experienced such intense pain as

when I saw that gun pointed at Beatrice. I held her in my arms, pleading for her not to die. Lying next to her on the carpet, now soaked with her blood, I whispered desperately, "Sweetheart, please don't leave me."

"Beatrice, I wanted to tell you that I love you—more than anything. I've always loved you, though it may be hard to believe. You're probably thinking, 'Is he crazy?' Yes, I am crazy because I've always loved you. You cannot die! Please fight to stay with me," I poured out my love for her, my voice filled with desperation and fear.

"Please let me know if you can hear me," I cradled her face in my hands, kissing her closed eyes and across her whole face. "Beatrice, sweetheart, please don't die. I don't want to live if you die. I love you so much."

"Hutch, let the firemen take care of Beatrice."

"What?"

"They are taking her to the hospital."

"I'll go with her," I said as I picked Beatrice up and gently laid her on the gurney the paramedics had brought into the bank. I couldn't recall them entering; my mind was focused solely on Beatrice. I refused to leave her side.

Amidst the tears of my mom, Sandy, and her girls, I scanned the room. Everyone was weeping, but I had to assert, "She's not dead. Stop acting like she is. She's going to be fine," I reassured everyone. *Beatrice wasn't dying; she was injured.*

I noticed her fingers moving when I spoke those words. "I told them, sweetheart. You're going to be fine. Did you hear me tell you I love you?" It was then I realized tears were streaming down my face like a waterfall onto Beatrice.

"Hutch, let them place her in the ambulance. I'll drive you to the hospital. You'll be right there with her," Ethan said, touching my arm. That's when I noticed the pregnant woman with blood all over her. There was a paramedic taking care of her.

"I'm riding in the ambulance," I declared loud enough for everyone to hear. I wasn't letting them take Beatrice away without me. I climbed into the ambulance, allowing the medical team to tend to her while I held her hand. The paramedic working on her appeared terrified. I pulled out my phone and dialed Griffin's number.

"I'm already here. Gray called me. I'm in the emergency room waiting for the ambulance."

"We're pulling into the hospital right now. You have to save her, Griffin. I can't lose Beatrice."

"I've got Angel Davis on his way. He'll be here soon. He was in Portland at the convention with me."

We arrived at the emergency entrance, they opened the ambulance's back doors, and Griffin pulled the gurney from the back, and they rushed off running with Beatrice. I ran right beside them until Griffin stopped me.

"Go home and shower and then come back. You are covered in blood."

"No, I'm not going to leave her."

"She'll be going into surgery."

"I'll wait in the waiting room."

I made my way to the waiting room. Gray was there. He tossed me a clean shirt. I threw mine into the garbage.

"How is she?"

"I don't know."

"Where did the bullet go in?"

"The side of her head. It's still in there. Angel Davis will be here soon. He and Griff were at a convention in Portland. I can't bear the thought of her not making it. I love her so much. Sometimes I despise myself for not going to her house when she was eight and apologizing for shouting at her."

"That's in the past. Besides, you did apologize. I remember when you were ten, and you told Bea you were sorry. Do you remember what she said?"

"Yes, I remember everything about Beatrice. She said, 'Thank you, but I already knew you were sorry.' Then she started crying and ran back to her classroom." I walked to where the surgery room was and leaned against the wall. I wanted to be here and nowhere else. "I'm going to wait right here."

"You know they are doing everything they can for Bea?"

"I know. I just want to stay here in case she needs me."

"I'll inform the others where you're at."

"Can you please not tell them exactly where I am? I know everyone loves Beatrice, but I would rather be alone. I don't think I could handle Mom's crying right now."

"Sure, I understand. Come to the waiting room when you feel up to talking to most of the town. Because they are all there waiting to see how she is doing."

After Gray left, I sat on the floor and prayed. I prayed that God would send down an Angel to save Beatrice. I was sitting with my head back and my eyes closed.

"What the hell are you doing?"

I opened my eyes. "Angel. Thank God you are here. Please save her."

"Do you love this woman?"

"More than anything in the world."

"Here, put these on and follow me. You are my assistant, don't talk to anyone else, and keep your mouth shut. You are there for moral support, and that's all."

I slipped into the clothes and mask Angel threw at me and walked behind him. I caught a glimpse of Beatrice on the bed, being prepared for surgery. Cassie, Lucy, and Griff glanced at me. I hoped the mask would cover my face enough so they wouldn't recognize me.

I glanced at Griff when he started talking. "Why the hell is he here?"

"He's here because he's my assistant." Griffin didn't say anything. My legs turned to jelly when I saw Beatrice lying on the bed, ready for surgery. I took her hand and kissed each finger. I remained motionless for hours as Angel extracted the bullet from her head. When they began, Lucy handed me a towel in case tears fell, but I didn't allow a single one. I stayed strong for my love.

Hours later, I saw Angel step back and stretch his neck. Cassie wiped his forehead and held up his water bottle with a straw for him to have a drink. Then he turned to me. "Hutch, the surgery went well. Now we wait for her to wake up and see how she is. I believe she's going to be fine. The next forty-eight hours will give us more clarity. My eyes started to burn, and I knew I would make a fool out of myself if I didn't leave. I nodded, and then I walked out. My body trembling with relief. She was still alive.

I leaned against the wall until I had myself under control. Wiping my eyes one last time, I made my way to the waiting room. Everyone stood up. I noticed Beatrice's parents among them. Walking over to them I took their hands. "Beatrice is going to make it. Angel said we needed to wait for the next forty-eight hours to be sure she would be fine."

"Thank God. I was so scared. My poor baby. I'll stay here and take care of her," Beatrice's mother said.

"You're welcome to stay here, but I will care for Beatrice. I love her, and I'm not leaving her side. Let's focus on getting her awake and assessing her condition. I'm sure she'll be here in the hospital for a while," I replied, glancing over at Gray and my mom.

"Do you want to tell us why you're dressed in doctor's clothes?" Mom asked as she rubbed my back.

"An Angel gave me these clothes so I could be by Beatrice's side during surgery.

∼

EIGHT DAYS LATER, Beatrice woke up, I was sitting in a chair beside her bed, engrossed in a book. As I glanced up, I noticed her observing me intently. "Sweetheart, thank God you are awake," I exclaimed.

"Sweetheart. Who are you talking to?" Her voice was hushed, but I could hear her.

"I'm talking to you."

"You must be joking. Why am I in the hospital?"

"There was a bank robbery, and you were shot. Why are you looking at me like that?"

"I'm trying to comprehend why you are here. Could I please have a drink of water?"

I was starting to feel uneasy about the way Beatrice was scrutinizing me. Shortly after I pressed the button, the nurse entered the room. "I see you've woken up. I'm glad to see that. How are you feeling?"

"Is my mother around."

"I'm not sure. Would you like me to call her?"

"Please."

"Beatrice, look at me. Why are you acting like you don't love me?"

"Did I tell you I loved you?"

"Not yet, but we're in love with each other."

"Why don't I remember us being in love?"

"Do you know who I am?"

"Yes, you are Hutch Campbell. I'm fairly certain this is the longest conversation we've ever had. Lordy, why don't you just poke me in the eyes with a stick? Because I'm pretty darn sure I can't get up and walk away."

"Why would I do that?"

"Because you hate me and never stay around me long enough for me to look at you. I don't want to do this." She closed her eyes and went back to sleep. I stood there until Griff came in.

"I thought she was awake."

"She just went back to sleep," I looked at him, "She doesn't remember us being together. She told me to poke her in the eyes with a stick because I've never been around her long enough for her to see me."

"I'm sure it's temporary."

"But what if it's not?"

"Then you make her fall in love with you again. Don't give up on her."

"I would never give up on her, and I won't let her chase me away. I love her, and she loves me. She'll remember. It'll take a few days, but I'll win her back."

"I hope so because if she wants you to leave this room, you'll have to leave."

"She won't ask me to leave. Beatrice loves me. She just doesn't want to admit it."

"I'm going to wake her. I need to see how she's doing. Why don't you wait over by the window?"

"This time I will because she doesn't remember us." I watched as Griff touched her and called her name.

"Bea, can you wake up for me."

"Griffin," I saw her look around. When she spotted me, I smiled.

"He said we were in love," she whispered, thinking I couldn't hear her.

"Yes, I understand you have a memory loss. What is the last date you remember?"

"Are you, my doctor? This feels kind of awkward having you as my doctor."

'Why is that?"

"Because I knew you in school."

"You are also a doctor of our schoolmate's children."

"Yes, their small children."

"So, you do remember you are a doctor."

"Of course, I remember I'm a doctor."

"What's the last thing you remember about Hutch?"

"I try not to remember anything about Hutch Campbell." I couldn't help but chuckle, and Beatrice turned and looked at me. "Why is he here?"

"Because he loves you. He's been here since you were injured."

"I don't remember any of that. How did we even start talking to each other?"

"You'll have to ask Hutch about that."

"I ran over to rescue you when two men broke into your house. You were shaken up and asked me to stay the night." She seemed skeptical. I could tell she was tired. "I'll get dinner, and you can talk to Griff. Beatrice, I know you'll remember. I love you. I've always loved you, and you've always loved me. I won't try and rush you. I'll see you tomorrow." She didn't say anything, and I walked out.

I would give her today, but I would return tomorrow.

15

BEATRICE

I watched Hutch walk from my hospital room, thinking that one of us was crazy, and I was pretty damn sure it wasn't me. My head throbbed painfully. I closed my eyes, and when I opened them again, a handsome man was checking my vitals. I watched him for a few minutes. "What is your name?"

Angel Davis, my specialty is head wounds. I'm a friend of the SEALs. I'm surprised Hutch isn't here. He was in the operating while I performed surgery on you."

"I don't remember there being an us."

"I wonder...."

"I don't know," I didn't let him finish talking, "I can't imagine there even being an 'us' with Hutch and myself. We haven't spoken since I was eight. We lived across the street from each other. Actually, he doesn't live there now. His mom still lives there."

"Why didn't you talk to each other?"

"It was a stupid reason. When I was little, I couldn't hold a heavy door open, and it slammed on Hutch's fingers. I laughed because that's what I did back then if I was scared or nervous. But I grew out of that. Thank God. He never spoke to me after that. Well, he did try to apologize to me. All I remember is I cried. The whole thing was stupid—wasted years.

"Oh my God, Hutch. How could I forget Hutch? I love him. I have to tell him." I started crying, and then my head felt like it would explode. I grabbed my head, and Angel began shouting for a nurse.

Amidst the chaos, I heard Hutch's voice, demanding to know what the fuck was happening. As the pressure in my head eased, I turned toward Hutch. "I'm so sorry. You're right I do love you; I just hadn't told you yet. I love you so much. I will always love you." Angel gave me a shot, and I didn't know anything after that.

16

HUTCH

I was in a state of panic as I watched my love suffer in immense pain. I turned toward Angel. "What happened," I asked Angel, desperately seeking answers.

"She was telling me about the two of you when you were little. She mentioned wasted years, and then she suddenly grabbed her head. She also remembered how much she loved you. I'm going to conduct an MRI. I need to see if something else is happening in her head that we might have missed. The severity of her headache suggests it's not a normal one.

I accompanied Angel and the X-ray technician as we wheeled Beatrice's bed down the hallway for her MRI. I anxiously waited outside the door until it was complete. When we returned to her room, Gilly was wiping her eyes.

"She remembers me, but Angel had to give her a shot because she was in so much pain," I informed Gilly embracing her.

"Have you seen Gray around here? I was supposed to meet him."

"No, I haven't seen him today."

"Here I am, sweets. How is Bea doing?"

"She remembers me, but Angel had to give her a shot because she was experiencing intense head pain. He's going over the MRI right now."

Just then Cassie walked into the room, Gray and Gilly exchanged glances. "Did you tell him?" Cassie asked.

"Tell me what?"

I looked at Gray, waiting for an explanation. He took a deep breath. "Bea is pregnant."

"What?" I exclaimed, shocked.

"She's about one month pregnant," Cassie confirmed.

"Who's pregnant?" Angel's voice echoed as he entered the room.

"They said Beatrice is a month pregnant," I whispered so I wouldn't wake Beatrice. I glanced at the bed and she was still sleeping.

"Hmm, her surgery is at six." I watched him shake his head. "We have to go back inside Beatrice's head. She had an aneurysm, and that's what caused all the pain. Fixing it won't take long. But if she is pregnant, we'll need to be extra careful with anesthesia."

"Do whatever you need to do to save Beatrice. She can have a baby anytime." I knew she was watching me. I looked down at her. "This baby is our first child. We will take special care to make sure our baby stays healthy. Angel, make sure my baby is safe; he's counting on his mommy to keep him safe. Hutch, we're going to have a baby. Will you marry me?" Cassie and Gilly laughed and clapped their hands.

"Yes, but I was going to ask you."

"Okay, you can ask me."

Angel laughed.

Beatrice looked over at Cassie and smiled. I knew she was tired; her eyes were almost closed.

"Cassie, have them put another bed in here for Hutch. He doesn't need to sleep in the chair."

"Beatrice, will you be quiet so I can ask you to marry me?"

"Yes."

"Beatrice Price, will you marry me and promise to love me forever?"

"Yes, Hutch, I will marry you. I love you so much." As I leaned in to kiss her, something went wrong. She grabbed for her head, cried out in pain, and closed her eyes. Cassie jumped on her bed, desperately trying to revive her.

"Do something, Angel. Please don't let her die." Time seemed to come to a standstill as we hurriedly pushed her bed back into the surgery room.

"This time, you stay in the waiting room," Angel said, turning to look at me.

I nodded, knowing this might be my last time to see Beatrice. I kissed her quickly before they pushed her through those doors. Making my way to the waiting room, I began to pray, acknowledging that I hadn't prayed enough in the past, wondering if God would even listen. But I was determined to beg him to remain by Beatrice's side during the surgery.

The next three hours felt like an eternity until Angel finally entered the waiting room. "She's going to be fine. We managed to repair the two veins that caused the aneurysm. Everything else looks good."

I had been sleeping on the cot Cassie brought to the ICU, where Beatrice was treated. The sound of voices woke me up, and I opened my eyes.

Beatrice looked at me and smiled. She was beautiful,

even with some of her hair shaved off on one side. "I'm sorry if I woke you. Both our moms insist we get married before the baby arrives. What do you think?" She asked.

"I think they are right. We'll get married once you are out of the hospital."

"What about my hair?" she inquired.

I smiled reassuringly. "What about your hair?"

"I don't want my wedding photos to show me with half of my hair shaved off."

"You'll look beautiful no matter how your hair looks," I said with genuine affection.

"I still can't believe these two are in love," Beatrice's mom remarked, observing us. "Do you remember how often I told you these two would make the perfect couple?" she asked, glancing over at my mom.

"Yes, but I never thought they would get together long enough to find out if it would work or not," my mom replied.

"I've always loved Beatrice. I realized I loved her when I was a sophomore in high school. I used to stand outside the music room and listen to Beatrice sing," I confessed.

"I had no idea," Beatrice said, surprised. I knew she needed to get some sleep.

"I was pretty pathetic, sneaking around just to hear you talking with your friends," I admitted. I liked seeing her smile.

"Why didn't you tell me? We could have been together much sooner."

"What matters is that we're together now," I assured her as I bent my head and kissed her.

"Yes, that's what matters. If I Occasionally look at you like I want to kill you, that'll be my old self. You can just ignore her," Beatrice said playfully.

"Okay, I will." I watched Beatrice close her eyes, falling asleep within seconds.

"I'll leave the two of you to take care of the wedding plans. Nothing extravagant, just family and a few close friends," I said, looking at both of them.

They had their heads together already planning when they left the room. I saw Beatrice's father standing in the doorway. "Hello," I greeted him, shaking his hand."

"I knew what was happening with my Bea when she was growing up. It wasn't lost on me that whenever there was a party at your house, there was also one at ours too. The kids split their time between the two houses. Beatrice has always had plenty of friends. I don't want you to feel bad about anything. I know you apologized to Beatrice a few times; she told me about it each time. She also told me she loved you when she was a junior in high school. I'm happy that the two of you found each other."

"Yes, we did." I replied, attempting to change the subject. "How is Florida?"

"We actually decided to move back here and bought a condo on the beach. It was going to be a surprise for Bea. We've been in Florida for eight years and still miss everyone in Cedar Falls—especially our baby girl."

"I'm glad to hear that. Beatrice will be so happy. You'll want to be with your grandchildren."

"Yes, we are looking forward to babysitting our grandkids."

"If you need help moving, all you have to do is ask."

"Thank you, but a moving company is taking care of everything for us. I didn't know how much work there was in moving until we moved to Florida. As you know, I grew up in Bea's home. But now I don't want all the work there is to taking care of a home and property as large as that house.

You won't have to worry about Bea has a company that takes care of everything weekly. I mean, if that's where you'll be living."

"I'll live wherever Beatrice wants to live. If you'll excuse me, I have to be at a meeting."

"Of course, I'll sit with Bea. You run along and take care of whatever you have to do. Beatrice will be fine."

I rushed out of there as quickly as possible. My anxiety was over the roof. I didn't comprehend the source of it, but when he started talking about the responsibility of caring for a yard, a heated pool, and where I would live, I found it difficult to breathe.

When I got home, I looked around. Since my home was on the beach, all I had was sand. The yard was a natural habitat. There wasn't much to do, clean a few weeds out occasionally and keep the trash picked up. It was so easy. But now everything would change. I would have a wife, a child, and a home that I was sure would need a lot more upkeep.

Of course, she has a company to take care of the upkeep, and I might even enjoy taking care of the pool and yard. I know I will love taking care of my baby and my wife. So, it's a win-win situation for me. I walked into the garage and took down some large containers that I had when I got out of the Seals. I decided to start packing some of my personal belongings.

Glancing at the clock, I left for the meeting. The office building where we had our own office boasted numerous plants, thanks to Sofie, Noah's wife, who had a green thumb and could grow anything. That explained the abundance of plants in my house. I made a mental note to take some of them over to Beatrice's house. She will love them.

Most of the guys were present, and a barbeque was in progress. The aroma of burgers filled the air, and I realized I hadn't eaten all day.

"How is Bea doing," Gray asked.

"She's doing great. She isn't too thrilled about her new haircut but she's doing great. She'll probably be able to come home in a few days. They don't like keeping you in the hospital for very long these days—it's in and out."

"Yep. So, you're getting married—the old ball and chain," Gray remarked.

I chuckled, knowing Gray loved his ball and chain. "Yep, just like my little brother."

Our kids will be playing together, just like we did when we were little. Mom says the wedding is next week in Beatrice's backyard."

My heart began to race with anxiety once more. "I didn't know it was next week. Why wasn't I informed? Next week wow."

"Hey, don't start panicking. This is what you wanted, remember? You love Bea, and the two of you will live happily ever after."

"I know all of that. I can't help it if my heart starts going into a panic. I'll have to report where I'm at all the time and ask if I can do something like go to Vegas for a weekend with my buddies. How do you pay the bills? Does she pay them, or do you pay them? I know nothing about being married."

"No one knows about marriage until you are married. You're going to love it. Stop worrying. You get to be with the woman you love. Besides, she also has to get used to all those things. You can do it together."

"You're right. I'm the luckiest man on earth. I'm marrying Beatrice Price, the love of my life. I'll let you men have this meeting without me while I visit the woman I love."

"Okay, we will see you later."

17

BEATRICE

I felt a sudden rush between my legs, and it didn't take but a second for me to realize what had happened. I turned to Stephanie, my voice trembling, "Something's not right. Can you help me to the bathroom? I just miscarried my baby," I choked out the words, tears streaming down my face. Cassie entered the room at that moment.

"What's going on?" she asked, coming to the side of the bed. "I had a miscarriage. I need to get to the bathroom," I said, desperately wanting to move quickly before Hutch walked in and saw me crying. My tears were uncontrollable, and my sobs echoed in the room.

I managed to make it to the bathroom before I heard Hutch enter. I tried to calm down, but my heart was broken. He came straight to the bathroom and gathered me into his arms while Cassie and Stephanie quietly left the room.

"What is wrong, sweetheart," he asked, his voice filled with concern.

"The baby is gone, and my heart is broken. I know he was a little embryo, but he was our embryo. I loved him so much. My body has been through so much it couldn't hold him in, so it released him," I whispered, my voice breaking.

"I'm sorry, sweetheart. We'll have more opportunities to have babies. I loved our baby too. Are you okay? Let me put you back to bed. Are you in any pain?"

"No, I'm not in pain. I just want to go home," I replied, wiping my tear-stained cheeks. I couldn't understand why I miscarried. In fact, I've only known about the pregnancy for one day. I wouldn't have known I miscarried if they hadn't told me I was pregnant. I would have thought I had a heavy period.

"They're discharging you tomorrow. We're are getting married next week," Hutch said.

I didn't feel ready to get married so soon. I just wanted to do nothing for a month or two to let my body heal. I at least wanted to let my hair grow out some. "We aren't having a baby anymore. You don't need to marry me," I said, my voice filled with uncertainty.

"Sweetheart, we're not getting married because of the baby. We're getting married because we are deeply in love. I love you, and that's why I want to marry you. I want to spend my life with you," Hutch tried to reassure me.

"I want to spend my life with you too, but I'd like to wait a few months. I want to be fully healed before we get married," I explained, hoping that Hutch would understand that he didn't have to rush into marriage.

"Baby, I don't want to wait. Let's do this. We love each other. Why do you want to wait?"

"I don't want to be unwell and have all these issues when we get married. So why don't we wait for just a little while? We haven't been dating for very long, and I don't want to feel like I've rushed you." I pleaded, hoping to relieve Hutch from feeling obligated to marry me.

"Why don't we keep dating, and then you can ask me to marry you in a few months if you still want to marry me."

"I'll agree to wait for two months and only two months. After that, I'll come crawling to you on my hands and knees, begging you to marry me. I'll have the wedding already arranged because we will get married the next day after I ask you."

"Okay, we can do that. Can you stay with me until I fall asleep?"

"Sweetheart, I'm staying the whole night. Why don't you get some sleep? I'm going to call our moms and talk to them about our wedding."

I woke up twice, and both times Hutch was lying next to me, he would pull me close, and I would drift back to sleep. I loved him deeply, but I felt like I needed to get away for some reason. Everything had been happening so quickly. Just two months ago, Hutch and I weren't even talking, and now we were on the path to getting married.

I didn't want Hutch to feel pressured into marrying me. We hadn't been dating for a long time, and it felt overwhelming. Despite knowing that I've always loved him, doubts began to creep into my mind.

"Sweetheart, relax," he whispered trying to calm me. I was sure he could feel my heart beating fast. "We don't have to rush into anything. We can enjoy dating and getting to know each other. As long as I can kiss you whenever I want, I'm happy. I love you. I'm sorry I didn't tell you in high school."

"I love you so much. I know it's better if we get to know each other," I whispered back.

A week had passed, and I decided to do something with my hair. Jenny assured me she could make it beautiful. I was surprised by the way she styled it. The shaved spot was completely hidden.

"Thank you so much, Jenny! I was freaking out about my hair, but now it looks amazing. I don't know how you did it but I love it."

"You have lots of hair so we could change the style and only had to cut a little off. Now when your hair starts growing, it'll just blend in."

"I told you Jenny could make it beautiful," Gilly said.

Gilly was on her own since Grayson had to leave for Kuwait to rescue a family that went missing. Hutch was upset over Grayson and Jackson going on their own because everyone else was occupied. I knew Hutch wanted to be with them but didn't want to leave me, even though I told him repeatedly that I was fine. In my heart, I was glad he didn't go there. The mere thought of him going to those dangerous countries scared me.

"Do you have time to cut and style my hair," Gilly asked.

"Of course! Have a seat, and I'll start on you right now."

"Gilly, I'll take the baby with me, and you can pick him up when you are finished."

"Thank you, don't forget the diaper bag. It has all of his things in it."

After leaving the Salon, I walked home with a smile on my face. The baby was such a joy, I couldn't help but laugh at his funny faces. I saw Hutch. As soon as I got on my road, he stood there waiting for me.

"How did you know I was walking home with this sweet baby?" I asked surprised.

"I didn't. I heard you laughing, and it sounded so sweet I went looking for you. You look beautiful, as always," Hutch said pulling me into his arms, he looked at the baby and laughed. The little guy was blowing spit bubbles.

"Your nephew is making me laugh." Hutch reached in and picked the baby up. Then he laughed, watching the baby make faces with his tongue.

"You are so funny. Let's take him inside before grandma sees him and snatches him away."

"I heard that! You stay right where you are. Grandma wants some kisses from her grandbaby," Hutch's mom playfully called out. We walked over to Hutch's mom's house so she could spend time with the baby. "I love your hair."

"Thank you, Gilly is getting her hair done now. She's upset that Grayson is overseas."

"It takes time to get used to having your family going overseas. I'm still not happy when the boys go there. I have to trust that they know what they are doing. I'm sure Grayson will be home in a few days," Hutch's mom assured me.

Two days later, Grayson went missing. Hutch was so distressed when he told me about his brother. "Jackson said he doesn't know how it happened. They were together, and Grayson got sick. Jackson went to find a doctor, and when he returned, the place was in chaos. Jackson has been searching everywhere for Grayson. I don't know how to tell you, but I have to leave to find my brother."

"I understand. I'm coming with you," I firmly declared.

"Sweetheart, hell no. You are not coming with me," Hutch declared, just as firmly.

"Yes, I am. I can be a great help to you. I'm a doctor. I'll gather my things," I insisted.

"Damn it, Beatrice, now is not the time for you to prove your stubbornness. Besides, I already know how determined you are."

"That won't change. I'm not arguing with you. When we arrive, you'll see that I'm

"Baby, I can't bring you with me every time I have to leave."

"I get that, but I have to come with you. I can feel it in my heart."

"The guys will kill me for taking you. Promise me you'll listen to everything I say. Can you do that?" Hutch asked, seeking reassurance.

"It' might be difficult, but yes, I can," I agreed.

"Alright, let's get our things ready. We leave at midnight," Hutch decided.

I wanted to jump with joy and clap my hands. I couldn't believe Hutch agreed to let me accompany him. Since most of his belongings were in my room, we went in together and packed what we needed.

18

HUTCH

I couldn't believe I had given in and allowed Beatrice to come along. The reason I relented was that I knew Beatrice would go on her own if I refused. We may not have been together for long, but I understood her. I knew everything about her. I had kept up on everything she did. I had kept up with her throughout the years since high school. I smiled and shook my head, remembering some of the things Jenny used to tell me.

"Why are you smiling?"

"Because I love you, and you managed to convince me to bring you along."

"I love you too," she responded, leaving out the latter part of my statement. I chuckled and pulled her into my arms.

WE ARRIVED in Kuwait at seven in the morning. I observed Beatrice as she stepped out into the scorching air. The sand seemed to instantly infiltrate our clothes and body. I watched as she took a breath and patted her chest, probably wondering how hot it could get out here. Without a complaint, she started walking. I knew she would never complain about the heat or anything else since she insisted on joining me.

I called Jackson to see where he was. He informed me that he was waiting for me at the airport. He wasn't thrilled when he saw Beatrice.

"Why the hell did you bring Beatrice? Are you fucking kidding me? You know there's a chance she might not make it back home. People are dying here at an alarming rate. They're attempting to take over the country," Jackson expressed his concern.

"Beatrice is a doctor, and she could be of great help to us. Do you have any idea where Gray is?"

"I know where he might be, along with the other missing people. We'll have to talk to someone. I'm waiting to hear back. However, it's going to be tricky. I don't trust anyone here. About twenty individuals have already been brutally murdered, leaving their bodies left hanging in the trees."

"Beatrice, did you hear what Jackson said?" I asked, wanting to ensure she understood the danger.

"I'd have to be deaf not to hear him. I'm standing right next to you."

"I just wanted you to understand that it won't be easy. It's incredibly dangerous. Why don't you wait at the hotel, and when we finish our business, I'll pick you up, and we can go home?"

"No, let's go. I came here to help you, and staying at the hotel won't accomplish that. Trust me, when I say I could be a valuable asset to your team."

"What are you talking about? You're not going to join our team. I brought you along because I didn't want your feelings to get hurt."

"You brought her to the Kuwait desert just to avoid hurting her feelings? Do you know how foolish that is?" Jackson interjected, questioning my decision.

"Yes, I know how foolish it was. What was I supposed to do, sneak off without her?

"Hell yeah, you're supposed to sneak off. We're not at some children's birthday party. People are missing, and the ones who took them are ruthless killers. They'd behead you if you didn't comply," Jackson countered, emphasizing the danger we faced.

"Instead of dwelling on what's already done, let's get out of here and find them. I turned towards Beatrice. Beatrice, it's crucial that you follow my instructions. This is not the time for stubbornness."

"What do you mean? I'm not stubborn."

Jackson and I chuckled. "Yes, you are," Jackson said, shaking his head. You have always been like this.

"Prove it. What have I ever been stubborn about? See, you can't think of anything."

"What about not talking to Hutch for all those years? Everyone blamed Hutch, but it was you."

"Jackson, it was both of us, and you know it. That's in our past. We're not discussing it anymore." She climbed into the back seat of the Land Rover. "Tell him, Hutch, that it was both of us, and it's in the past. We're done with it."

"Yes, Jackson, that's in the past. We're not talking about it anymore. Just because you've known Beatrice since she was a baby doesn't mean you can argue with her. Beatrice and I have resolved it, so let's change the subject."

. . .

"WHAT ARE YOU TALKING ABOUT? I was with you three times when you tried apologizing to her. She would look at you her bottom lip trembling, turn around, and walk away."

"That's because I knew I'd start crying if I didn't walk away, and everyone would see how much of a baby I was."

Jackson persisted, "Why would you start crying?"

"Because I wanted to be good friends with Hutch and I accidentally smashed his fingers. I knew he hated me. I knew his Mama probably told him to apologize for yelling at me, and I was embarrassed because I couldn't even hold the door open. I'm not discussing it anymore. Talk to the corner of the wall if you have something to say about that incident because I'm not listening. Hutch and I are done with it. He loves me, and you and the others need to stop bringing up the past."

"I'm sorry, Bea. I'm not trying to be mean. I'm just so upset that Gray is missing. Hell, everyone is missing. I don't even know how they were kidnapped."

"Maybe Gray decided to get caught so he could find the missing family," she said, wiping her brow, where all the sweat was running into her eyes. She took a handkerchief from her bag and tied it around her forehead.

"Do you have any more of those handkerchiefs?" She took it out of her bag and handed it to me. I tied mine as Beatrice did. I didn't even mind the little flowers on it. It kept the sweat out of my eyes. I saw Jackson eying us. Beatrice took out another one and handed it to him, pink and baby blue. I had to bite my tongue to hold back a laugh.

"I think Beatrice might be right. That sounds just like something Gray would do."

"I should do that," Beatrice said, looking at both of us seriously.

"Are you freaking crazy? Do you really think I would let

you get caught just so you could see where they were? What good would that do?"

"I've tried telling you I'm an expert in martial arts."

"Why didn't you take down those two guys who broke into your house?"

"I would have, but then you were there, and they were both down. Did I ever thank you for that? I should thank those men for breaking into my house and Adam for calling you. We have a lot of people to thank for bringing us together," Beatrice replied, with a giggle escaping her. "Gabe thinks he was the one to bring us together."

Jackson chuckled as he climbed into the truck. "Only you would want to thank the damn people who broke into your house," Jackson said, smiling. I had to hold in the laugh that tried to escape when I looked at Jackson.

"What is so funny," I asked her.

"You two are so pretty." We all laughed.

We had driven for forty-five minutes when Jackson pulled into a driveway. "Where are we staying?" I asked.

"This house belonged to the missing family. Her mother gave us a key to stay here. The man is Don, whose family is paying us to find this missing family. The husband is American, and the wife is Syrian. They said they have no political ties at all."

"Do you think her family is telling the truth? They can't be happy that she married an American."

"No, they are scared to death. They don't know what's going on. The wife was once engaged to someone else, but she fell in love with her husband when she moved to America. But that was ten years ago, and they don't think he would have anything to do with it," Jackson replied.

"Did you get his name?" I asked.

"Yes, it's Bader Salib. He lives in New York. Sofie is

checking him out. She'll contact us as soon as she has any information," Jackson informed me.

"It wouldn't make any sense why they would take Gray?" I voiced my confusion.

"I don't know," Jackson admitted.

"The only way we can catch them is if they catch me," Beatrice interjected.

"Beatrice, you promised to do what I said," I reminded her.

"I am doing just that. All I did was suggest something to you. All you have to do is say no, which is what you did," Beatrice defended herself.

"Sweetheart, do you remember you were close to death? I couldn't bear it if something happened to you, and you know that's the truth," I said, kissing her lips.

"I know. I'm sorry. I just thought I could be more helpful. I'll take my bag to the bedroom. Do you know where I'm going to sleep?"

"I sleep in the front room. You can pick any room you want. There are four bedrooms here."

"I'll find us one," I said, taking my sweetheart's arm. "I think this room will be perfect for us," I said, setting our bags on the bed. "Beatrice, please don't make me regret bringing you. I swear if I have to tie you up, I will. I'm going to go with Jackson. We have to question some people, but I'll be back. I don't want you to leave this house and keep the doors locked.

"I promise I won't go anywhere. I'll keep the doors locked. I won't talk to anyone if somebody rings the doorbell. I won't even look out the peephole. You won't have to worry about me, I promise. I'll cook us dinner while you are gone," Beatrice assured me.

"You don't have to cook dinner unless you want to. We

won't be gone long," I said, pulling her into my arms and kissing her deeply. "I love you so much."

"I love you too. Okay, I'll stay here, but be careful. I don't want you to go missing too. Maybe I should go with you," Beatrice hesitated.

"No, you should stay here until I get back," I insisted, kissing her again, and we left to talk to someone Jackson said might information about what was going on and where Grayson was.

The place we were sent to was a hellhole. I felt like they were after money and thought to get some by claiming to know what was happening. We talked to three different men before a woman approached us.

"You give me one thousand dollars, and I will take you to where they are held captive," the woman proposed.

I looked at Jackson, unsure of what to do. "How far away is this place?" I asked cautiously, sensing a possible scam.

"Not far. We will ride with you," she replied.

"No, we will follow you," I countered.

"We have no vehicle," she explained, initiating an argument with the men, in a language we couldn't understand.

"We will take you, but we'll stop a block away, and we want our money before we leave.

"We'll give it to you when you show us where this place is. We have five hundred dollars. Take it or leave it. We have other people who said they would show us the spot," I lied, testing her reaction.

More arguing ensued, and eventually, she nodded. "I know you are lying, but they want to take the five hundred," she admitted. We followed them to an even worse-looking area than we were in. They pulled over, and she approached my window.

"There is a house down there that has a purple door.

Everyone calls it the purple-door house. That is where your friend is. I don't know if the missing family is with them. I haven't heard anything about them."

I believed her. I gave her five hundred and then another five hundred. "This is yours," I said. She stuffed it in her blouse and hurried back to the men.

We decided not to drive the rest of the way, so we walked. "Are you sure she was telling the truth?" Jackson asked again.

"I think she was," I replied, trying not to draw attention to ourselves but being over six feet tall with broad shoulders. It was hard not to stand out.

"There is the purple door. Let's see if we can see through the windows," I suggested as we ran to the side of the house. That's when I heard someone shouting, I knew it was Gray. I ran to the front and kicked the door open. I didn't see anyone; no killers jumped out at us.

"Here he is," Jackson shouted, finding Gray.

"Thank God you two are here. Those men were going to the house they said to kill the Americans. Hutch, when did you get here?" Gray asked.

"A few hours ago," I stood frozen. "What house are you talking about?" I asked, my voice trembling.

"That house we are staying at," Gray replied. I roared so loud that the windows shook. As I ran back to get the truck, I pulled up in front of the house with the purple door for Gray and Jackson helped Gray into the backseat. I didn't even ask about his injuries.

"How do you feel," I asked Gray as the truck sped through the streets.

"I'm fine. Tell me why you are so upset," Gray inquired.

"Because Beatrice is at that house. How many men were there? Maybe she hid somewhere," I panicked. The next thirty minutes felt like an eternity. My heart pounded in my chest. As soon as the truck stopped, my door was opened. I saw the mess inside the house, and my heart pounded so hard I couldn't stop shaking.

"Beatrice, sweetheart, where are you? My heart raced as I called out for Beatrice. Beatrice, sweetheart, where are you?" I shouted louder than the last time.

"Why are you shouting? I'm cooking dinner," she replied calmly, walking into the hallway.

"Who tore the house up?"

"Those men who came here tore it up. I don't like hurting people, but they left me no choice," Beatrice explained.

"What?" I exclaimed, shocked.

"Gray, look at you. Hutch, get him a chair," Beatrice said, concerned.

"Beatrice, you have a fucking black eye," I said, taken aback.

"They snuck up on me, so I was shocked there momentarily," she explained.

"Sweetheart, when did they leave?" I asked, worried.

"They didn't leave. They are in the living room. I had to put tape on their mouths, they wouldn't shut up, and I had dinner cooking."

"We walked into the living room, and to our surprise, all three men were tied up with tape covering their mouths. I looked over at Gray and Jackson, "I told you, she was a martial art expert," Gray said, sitting in a chair.

"Do you think you can have them tell us where the family is?" Gray asked Beatrice.

"No, she can't get them to tell us anything. We'll make them tell us."

"They told me the family was home. It's the only way they could leave without her family stopping them. The family wanted them always to live here, but she wanted her kids to grow up in a free world. That's what the woman told them."

"What about his family? Do they know that their son and his family are home safe? None of this makes sense. I can't imagine the man would know where his son is. He pays us big money for hunting for his son. He would call off the hunt if he knew where his son was."

"I asked them that same question. They don't know anything about the family. Maybe you should call his family, and they can check for themselves if what these men say is true."

"That's what we'll have to do. So, how were you able to converse with the men?" I asked as I pulled Beatrice close to me for a kiss.

"I speak six different languages. I did tell you I would be able to help you."

"How the hell did you manage to do this?" I said, waving my hand at the three men tied up.

"Well, when that one punched me," I looked over at the guy she pointed to, and he knew he was getting his face smashed in. "I was able to knock one out right away. They were not expecting me to fight back. It took me a while to get the other two. But I was sure I could do it. Just let me get out of here before you let them loose because they said they would kill me."

"They will regret ever saying that to you, Sweetheart."

19

BEATRICE

I was checking out Gray's wounds. They looked very painful. "I wouldn't mind learning some of that martial arts stuff," Gray said, looking at me. "Not that I wouldn't be able to take out those three men if they hadn't snuck up on me and hit me over the head."

"Of course, you would have," I said, hoping he didn't see me roll my eyes.

"But I want to learn how you knocked them out long enough to tie them up. Is there a pressure point that you squeeze or something?"

"Yes, it's or something. It takes a lot of training to reach those skills."

"Can't you just show me how it's done?"

"It's not as simple as that. You should have stayed in the class when you were little, and you would have known all of this. I remember you and Hutch were in the class for about two months, and then you both quit. Griffin stayed in the longest, I remember that he was there even when he was injured. He only quit because he had a broken arm. Wasn't he always getting something broken? What was his family like? Do you think he was mistreated?"

"Sweetheart, Griff doesn't like talking about when he was growing up. He was taken away from his father when he was thirteen. He moved in with us."

"That's right, I remember now. He used to come over, and I would show him the moves I had learned. And the next thing I knew, he was gone. Where did he go?"

"He found his grandma. She took him home with her. They became very close. After he got out of the SEALS, he lived in Hawaii. The place was beautiful, far away from everything. It was off the grid. He did have some solar, but not much. He comes and goes from here and there. We keep waiting for him to settle down here. I think he has such bad memories for him. He doesn't like staying in Cedar Falls longer than he has to."

"Oh my God, I hope I don't start crying when I see him. Where is his father?"

"He died, like, fifteen years ago. There was not one person at that man's funeral. Griffin went there and spit on his grave. Do not ever tell Griffin we talked about this."

"Don't worry. I won't say anything. I'll show you how to take men out quickly, but you will have to keep practicing. It's not something you learn overnight."

"Okay, I'll do what you say. We quit because it was stupid and boring. We never got to fight with our friends using karate or learn any fighting skills. The teacher was only teaching us how to bow and different ways to move our hands. Shouting that loud noise. I still don't know why that was so important."

"Maybe you can show all of us how it's done?" Hutch said as he and Jackson walked into the room where I checked his brother for injuries.

"Sure, I'll teach all of you at the same time. But you have to realize that it's not something you learn overnight. It took me years to learn this technique."

"We understand," Jackson said with a snicker. *Showing Jackson a few of my techniques will give me great pleasure.*

"Is there a spot on their shoulders where you put pressure on it, and they go to sleep?"

I couldn't help myself; I laughed. "You've watched too many Bruce Lee movies. There is not a spot on the shoulder that puts them to sleep. You have to use strength and knowledge to knock them out cold. What are we going to do with them?"

"Someone is on their way here to pick them up. I put in a call to the man who hired us. He was going to see if his son was home. If he is, then we'll go home today," Hutch said looking at the bruises on Gray's back.

After dinner, I took a shower and went to bed. I felt the mattress sag when Hutch got in. I turned toward him for a cuddle. "How is Gray doing?"

"He's in pain, but those Tylenol you gave him helped. He pulled me into his arms. How do you like this business?"

"I'll stick with my job. I see some bad stuff, but your work deals with too much mayhem and killings. Has the father called yet?"

"His son wasn't at home, but he called his father. He said his wife's family tried to kill him. He finally found help so his family could leave the country. He's still hiding because he doesn't know if anyone is still after him."

"That's crazy. So, the woman who gave the keys to Jackson is the one who wants him dead. Don's mother-in-law. I've heard about scary mothers-in-law, but this woman might be the worst." It was hard for me to concentrate, much less talk, with Hutch pulling my tee shirt and panties off. He was already naked and very ready to make love to me. I found that out when I ran my hand over his body.

"Hey baby, you feel wonderful," he ran his hands down my legs. I may have moaned. He covered my lips with his mouth as he pulled me on top of him. My fingers pushed through his hair as the kiss deepened. "I've been wanting to do this all day."

"You feel pretty good yourself. I said as my hands caressed his back. My touch was feather-light until he kissed me again. My touch quickly became more frantic. I clutched his shoulders, demanding for him to stop tormenting me.

"Hutch" I didn't know if I shouted his name or sighed it. His hands had moved between my thighs, driving me out of my mind. Hutch knew just where to touch, exactly how much pressure to exert. I pleaded for him to come to me.

I was desperate to feel every inch of him, to wrap myself in his warmth. His breathing became more labored, and that excited me even more. If he continued to torment me, I thought I might just die.

Hutch delayed as long as he could, wanting to give me as much pleasure as possible. But my response made it impossible for him to wait any longer. I was practically begging him to make love to me. Our mouths connected and he moved between my thighs, slowly sinking into me. I was so ready for him, and he groaned as he sank deeper inside me. He stayed completely still, panting and whispering my name.

As he started moving, I cried out, overwhelmed by ecstasy. "Ah, Beatrice." He whispered my name again. "Damn."

I wasn't content to let him catch his breath. Every nerve in my body was yearning for release. I lifted my knees urging him to go deeper, and began to move.

Oh, how I wanted to please Hutch and drive him as wild as I was. I kissed his mouth and then his ear before I moved to his neck. Panting, I felt his thrust go deeper, and tears filled my eyes. The intensity of the sensations building inside me was staggering. His movements became more powerful, demanding, and all-consuming. It was exquisite, wild, and beautiful, my heart expanded with love so powerful.

Even in the throes of raw passion, Hutch had always maintained control during our lovemaking. But now he couldn't control anything. I was learning more about the depths of the man I loved. He thrust into me again and again, powerless to slow down.

I matched his passion with my own. Tension built within me, yearning for release. We moved like wild animals taking and giving. Wave after wave of sensation washed over me. Leaving me breathless. I allowed myself to be swept away, like a rollercoaster plummeting to the ground, electrifying every nerve. The pleasure coursing through me was overwhelming, and tears of love streamed down my face. This man, was finally mine.

Hutched kissed me muffling my cry of ecstasy, then kissed away my tears, burying his face in the crook of my neck, and I couldn't help but chuckled. "Damn, Hutch, you're going to kill me."

Hutched laughed. "We'll kill each other, sweetheart." I nodded before my eyes closed.

I felt a light slap on my butt, and then Hutch kissed my neck and whispered, "Time to get up, sweetheart."

That jolted me awake, and I sat up so quickly that I lost my balance. Hutch caught me before I could fall off the bed. "Here is your coffee."

"Are we going home?"

"We're are going to guard Don and his family. His mother-in-law has hired hitmen. I don't want you anywhere near men with rifles."

"I need to go with you. What if someone shoots you?"

I'll be fine. Don't worry about me. I know what I'm doing. I want you to be safe so I don't have to worry about you." I noticed he was smiling as he watched me dress. So, I looked down and laughed. "See what you do to me," I had my bra on over my blouse.

I love you, baby, and I'll always love you. But you have to go home and let me do my job."

I know. Let me get my things together. I'm going to miss you. If you ever need a doctor, just say the word, and I'll be there." He pulled me into his arms and kissed me. "You know something. I haven't thought about my hair once since I've been here," I said as he rested his forehead against mine.

"It's beautiful, just like you."

"Yeah, right," I said as I walked to the mirror. We both laughed when I saw him looking at me through the mirror. My hair was a mess, and it stuck out everywhere. I remembered going to bed with it wet. That was a habit I needed to break if I wanted to always look good for my man. I laughed out loud, knowing that would never happen.

20

HUTCH

I watched Beatrice as we got on the plane. I knew she wanted to go with me, but it wouldn't be safe. I could tell she was worried about me, but this was my job and she would have to get used to it. I couldn't risk her life just because we would miss each other. The love I have for her is so powerful. I would never take a chance that something would happen to her. Bringing her this time was a mistake. She could be dead right now if she didn't know how to fight. Gabe was meeting us at the airport in Florida, where he would accompany us, and Beatrice and Gray would go home.

"Hutch, I'm going to miss you," Beatrice said, laying her head on my shoulder.

"I'll miss you too, sweetheart. Maybe this will be over soon. I want us to marry when I get home," I said, kissing her forehead.

"I'll have everything ready for when you get home."

Two weeks later, I was ready to strangle Don's wife. She kept going outside where anyone could see her. After the third time, I decided to talk to her husband. "I want to ask you a few questions. I don't want you to get angry. Just answer them truthfully."

"Why wouldn't I answer them truthfully?"

"Do you have a life insurance policy on yourself?"

"Yes, I do."

"How much is it?"

"I think it's five hundred thousand dollars."

My left brow went up. "But you don't know? Call right now and see what it is. Don't tell anyone."

"Okay," Don took out his phone and called. I noticed the surprise on his face as he hung up, and looked at me. "Five million dollars. He said Seri changed it six months ago because she was worried about skyrocketing prices. Why didn't she tell me?"

"We believe your wife is in on this with her mother."

"She loves me. Seri would never hire someone to kill me. Would she?"

"It happens all the time. I'm going to separate you and the kids away from Seri. We won't say anything until it's done. Do you know where she is?"

"Do you think she would harm the children?"

"Does she have a life insurance policy on them?"

"Yes, I just found out she does, two million dollars each."

I think you and the kids need to get away from your wife until we figure this out."

"I was fucking blind. It's all coming together now. It wasn't her mother, it was Seri. Her mother called me and told me she needed me and the kids to visit her. This was when we were in Kuwait, but Seri overheard us, and she convinced me that all the accidents I was having were because her mother wanted to kill me and keep Seri and the children in Kuwait. Her Mom was going to tell me, but we snuck away before she could.

"Go quietly, get the kids. Their bags are still in the vehicle. Take them to the garage, and get in the car, and I'll be there in a few minutes. I have to tell Gabe what's going on. Act normal, for Christ's sake," I said, trying to keep Don calm. We didn't know what his wife would do. She could kill all of us and say it was the men her mother hired.

I found Gabe and told him about the situation. He suggested taking Jackson with me and he would stay to keep an eye on Seri. We decided to meet in Sedona instead of going to Alaska.

"You'll have to be careful. We don't know if she has a gun or what the hell she has. Don't eat anything she cooks. Stay watchful. She might sneak the men in here. Jackson and you both can stay with the woman."

"Okay, you be careful."

"I will be," I grabbed my bag and headed to the garage. They were waiting for me. I climbed into the driver's seat and looked at everyone. "Let's go."

Three weeks later, we were still trying to catch Seri. An FBI agent was assisting us in setting up a plan to catch her in the act of hiring someone to kill Don. Don was still in shock, unable to believe that his wife could want him dead. I explained to him that money could change someone in an instant.

"Yes, but she never once acted like she wanted me dead. We never argued," Don said still trying to comprehend what was going on.

"That should have told you something right there. Spouses argue you can't agree on everything. It means she didn't have any opinions of her own, or you agreed with everything she said?" I pointed out.

Don was shaking his head, He looked like crap. "She never did express an opinion on anything," he said, "I thought it was because that's how she was raised. And since she never said anything, I guess I thought she loved me and agreed with what I said. Fuck I was so stupid. Why did I never question anything."

"Because you thought everything was perfect. There was no reason to question anything. If we hadn't found out about the life insurance, we still wouldn't know anything," I reassured him, I didn't mention he would probably be dead right. I was ready to go home. I missed Beatrice more than I have ever missed anyone.

That was the thing with Beatrice; I always knew I would be seeing her when I came home. When I came home from college on holidays, she would be home. When I entered the service, I wondered who she was with. I always heard how she was doing from my mom, and Jenny. I guess they knew what I wouldn't admit out loud. I loved Beatrice Price.

All the time we were away from each other, I knew I loved her. I just didn't acknowledge it. But I do now. I've called her about six times, even though that was frowned upon. I called her anyway. I couldn't wait for us to get married and have children—beautiful little girls who looked just like her.

I started panicking because I realized you had to watch out for who your children married. I called Beatrice. "Hey, sweetheart, I just realized that we'd have to investigate all of our children's dates when they start dating." I heard her chuckle, and I became hard. "I love you and miss you so damn much."

"I love you too," she whispered.

"Are others around you?"

"I'm in a meeting, but I'm so happy you called."

"I love you, Beatrice Price. Goodbye."

"I love you, Hutch Campbell. Goodbye."

I smiled as I hung up the phone, wondering who else was in the meeting. Now they can let the town know that Beatrice Price told Hutch Campbell she loved him in a room full of people. I jumped ten feet when I heard the scream. The small child ran to me, screaming she was covered in blood. I quickly scooped her up searching for her injury, but there was none.

"Listen to me. I want you to stay in here and keep the door locked," I said urgently, turning on the light as I put her in the closet with the lock. I rushed outside and saw the boy lying in a pool of blood. Jackson was shot, as was the child's father. Gabe picked up the child and ran inside. I grabbed Don and saw Jackson getting up. Then he fell back down. I hurried with Don and ran back and got Jackson.

"What the fuck happened?"

"He opened the gate for his fucking wife," Jackson shouted, "That fucker called her and told her where we were," Jackson shouted, again.

I grabbed the boy and ripped his shirt off, and he was barely breathing. I called Beatrice. I need your help. The child has been shot in the hip. He's lost a lot of blood and barely breathing. The ambulance is on its way. Beatrice, I need to keep him alive. Tell me what to do."

"I'm going to video call you. Hang up."

"My phone rang. I quickly turned on the video call and saw my baby. "Let me see his wound."

"He's lost a lot of blood."

"You have to tie a tourniquet around the top of his leg. See if there is a tie or rope anything just hurry. Find a white cloth and wash the area thoroughly. We must ensure that nothing enters his wound. Hutch, you are doing great. Are there any other injuries?"

"Jackson and the father, the little girl, is scared, but she's okay," I looked over at the father and he was staring into space, as if he was still in shock.

Jackson shouted, and I turned to see three men and Don's wife in the backyard. I grabbed my gun and fired. Two men fell, but I felt a bullet nick me. I heard Beatrice scream as she witnessed me being shot.

"I'm okay, sweetheart, it's just a little scratch on my arm. Don't worry; Gabe went after him. Beatrice, sweetheart, calm down. I'll be fine." I heard the ambulance and the police sirens outside.

As I turned around, another gunshot pierced my chest. Beatrice's scream echoed, but there was nothing I could do. I collapsed, and the phone slipped from my hand. All I could think was that I wouldn't let this kill me. I faintly heard another gunshot and Gabe's furious roar.

21

BEATRICE

My heart pounded hard when I saw that bullet strike Hutch, and he flew back onto the sofa. I feared he was dead. I continued screaming until Jackson grabbed the phone up off the floor. "Bea calm down. He's not dead, for God's sake. Stop screaming."

"Check if he's breathing. Feel for a pulse. Do something! Oh God, please don't let him be dead. Please don't let him be dead. Can you feel anything? Jackson, say something. Answer me, damn it! Is there a pulse?"

"Yes, I can feel a slight pulse. Bea, I have to hang up. There's too much to do. I don't have time to talk right now."

"I'm coming up there. Tell me where you are."

"We are in Sedona, Arizona. Call Ryker, and he'll bring you here in our plane."

Thank God all I had to do was push a button to call Ryker. My hand trembled as I sobbed uncontrollably. Ryker answered after half a ring.

"I'm already on my way. Where are you?"

"I'm at home. I already packed my bag. I saw Hutch get shot. Ryker, Hutch told me the husband called the wife and revealed their location. He thought he could talk her out of harming him and the kids. That bastard deserves to die. His son is severely injured; I was on the phone with Hutch when she shot him. The boy was shot in the hip. He lost so much blood." I kept talking until he pulled in my front yard, and he listened.

It took two hours to get to the airport in Sedona and another hour to drive to the hospital. When we arrived Hutch was in surgery I didn't waste any time seeking permission. I put on a surgical gown and walked into the operating room where Hutch was.

No one was going to chase me out of there. I was prepared to fight anyone. I observed for a while before squeezing my way in there and helping the doctor with the surgery. I saw him making too many sloppy mistakes. Hutch underwent surgery for seven hours.

I stepped into the waiting room and looked at his friends. "Now we wait. We'll know how he's doing within twenty-four hours. How's Jackson doing?"

He's doing well. They removed the bullet from his leg. They said he would have to stay a few nights. The little boy will make it, thanks to the tourniquet Hutch applied," Ryker said as he walked up to me and hugged me. You know how strong Hutch is. He knows you are here waiting for him. He won't let a bullet kill him. He's waited too long for the two of you to be together. So, don't make yourself sick over this.

I smiled at Ryker. I never thought you'd be playing the role of my dad. I wonder if your kids love you so much because you're the best dad." And then I broke down crying. "Why does this keep happening? When will we have a normal life?"

"Just one year, without anything crazy happening. I want Hutch by my side. Is that too much to ask for? I'm telling you right now, Ryker, when he gets out of here Hutch is taking a break. No one better ask him to go anywhere unless I'm with him. I'm going to see Jackson. Who wants to go with me?" Both Gabe and Ryker stood up to go with me. "We'll sneak in and see Hutch after we visit with Jackson."

I fell asleep in the waiting room; someone must have covered me up. When I woke up, Ryker and Jackson were sleeping. I turned my head as I heard someone clearing their voice. Hutch's mom Hellen and his brother Gray were sitting in the chairs.

"Have you heard anything?" I asked, my throat sore from crying.

"Not yet. We would love to visit him. Do you think you could get us in there?"

"Follow me," I said standing up. I was attempting to tame my natural curly hair. That was the thing with natural curly hair, it had a mind of its own. Gray put his arm around me, and Helen went to the other side and put her arm through mine. That is how we walked into the hospital intensive care unit where Hutch lay still sleeping.

I glanced at his chart, not much had changed. That's good," I whispered. Tears welled up in my eyes, and Hellen enveloped me in her arms. "Hutch is fighting like crazy to stay with you. He has loved you all his life. The two of you just took the long way to find all this out. Hutch will wake up soon. He doesn't want to see the woman he loves crying."

"I know. I don't mean to cry. Tears fall out when I'm unaware of it."

"That's okay, sweetheart, but I want you to know I'm going to be fine. It would help me a lot if you didn't worry about me. How is the little boy?" Hutch's voice filled the room surprising all of us.

"He's doing good. You saved his life when you put that tourniquet on his leg."

"You saved his life by telling me to put it on him. I was dreaming about him. I dreamed he was running with his sister playing in a field of flowers." We heard a noise and turned; a man stood there watching us. I quickly dried my eyes.

I'm the grandfather to the children. I don't know how to thank you for saving my grandchild. They will be going home with my wife and me. Our son is too stupid to raise children."

"I told him the first time I met his wife, that she would stab him in the back. I can't understand why he would bring that bitch and her killers to where the children were kept in a safe house. I'm sorry, but when I heard what he had done I was furious and I still haven't shaken it off."

"He must have thought she would see him and realized she loved him. That's the only thing I was able to come up with," I said, taking Hutch's hand in mine.

"I guess. This is for Seal Security," he said, handing over a large envelope.

A nurse came running in and told the grandpa that he was needed. Hellen and I stayed with Hutch while Gray followed the nurse and grandpa.

"Crawl up next to me, sweetheart. I've missed you so much," Hutch whispered as I sat beside him.

"Hutch, I can't crawl up there next to you. You've just had a bullet taken out of your chest. I don't think it will do you any good for me to snuggle with you. I have missed you so much, too," I replied, my voice trembling with emotion.

"I'll let you two have some time together," Hellen said, walking away. Hutch patted the bed, and I climbed up next to him.

"Beatrice, I would never let anything keep me from returning to you. I've waited a long time for us to be together. I know you were scared that I wouldn't come back to you. I'm here and will always be right next to you. We have a life with children coming soon, and I would never take that away from you. Is it okay if I go back to sleep?"

"Yes, shut your eyes." As soon as he drifted off to sleep, I got up. I had so much planning to do. The first thing I did was visit Jackson. "How do you feel?"

"I feel like I'm ready to go home. How is Hutch?"

"Hutch is doing great. I have something to ask you."

"Ask away."

"Will you please sing at my wedding?"

"Are you frigging crazy? Hell no, I won't sing at your wedding. I don't know how to sing."

"We both know that's a lie. I heard you singing a few times. There is no reason to pretend you can't sing just because you didn't know I listened to you."

"Bea, you have to drop this. Just because I sang in high school doesn't mean I can sing. One time when I was in the service, I got up in front of a crowd of people at a club and froze. I couldn't say a word. I stood there as they waited for me to sing. Finally, Gabe came up and walked me off stage. He made a joke, and they laughed. I never went back to that club

"Yeah, I remember that," Gabe said, laughing. "I never tried talking Jackson into singing at a club again. The reason I wanted him to sing was because of the competition."

"Now I remember it was that damn competition. How could I forget it was the Green Berets? Smoke would sing against me, and whoever won would win this giant jar filled with cash. After I froze, he didn't have to sing because we had to forfeit the bet. But he got up there and sang anyway, and he was good."

"I bet you are even better, so what do you say are you going to sing at my wedding?"

"No."

"Oh, sing at her wedding, for Pete's sake," Ryker said, walking into the room. "I'm sure you've outgrown your stage fright. Why don't you sing at Bea's and Hutch's wedding, and Bea can sing at yours."

"I'm never getting married. Why would I screw up the perfect life by getting married? Hell, it makes me sick thinking about it. I'm not talking about you and Hutch. Hell, we all knew you two would get married. Even when you were not talking to each other, we knew because Hutch spent most of our visit to his house staring over at your house, and every time we were around, you were always asking how everyone was. We all knew who you were asking about."

"Why didn't you tell me? We could have already been married."

Jackson shrugged his shoulders. "We discussed that, but then you two wouldn't have found each other."

"I swear, sometimes you guys make me want to cry."

"I can't believe you have any tears left. You haven't stopped crying since we got here," Ryker said, smiling.

"I know I have the worst headache. So, please tell me you will sing at my wedding."

"Damn, okay. But if I screw this up, it's on your head. I'll pick the song. You just let me know the date."

"Thank you, I hugged him. Something wasn't right. My hands felt his face. Then I pulled the blanket back.

"What are you doing?"

"Your hot."

"Why thank you, honey, you're pretty damn hot yourself."

"Not that kind of hot. Damn, you have an infection.

Jackson watched every move I made. "What are you going to do?"

"This will hurt you more than it does me. So stay still. Ryker hold his leg down. I have to open these stitches back up. We all looked at his wound. It was red and swollen with puss leaking out of it. Gabe, get that clean washcloth and run it under hot water."

"I have to draw that infection out. I don't want the surgeon to have to cut your leg off."

"Fuck, get all of that poison out of there. I knew it felt hot. Someone get me some antibiotics."

I snipped the stitches, and the poison squirted out as soon as it opened. "Let's leave this open for a bit. Has it been hurting you?"

"Well yeah, but it hasn't been long since they sewed it up. I thought it was natural that it hurt. I mean, it's a bullet hole. Of course, it hurt."

"Well, now you can get better." I'm going back to Hutch. I'll stop at the nurse's station and explain what happened."

"Bea, thank you."

"You're welcome."

22

HUTCH

Finally, we were on our way home, after five long days. Jackson required a longer stay because his leg wasn't healing properly and he was afraid of losing it. That's why we all stayed in Sedona, Arizona. It didn't make sense to us why Jackson panicked at the thought of Beatrice leaving, It was because Beatrice found the infection
. Now here we found ourselves lying in bed, with Jackson in another room of Beatrice's house refusing to leave until his wound heals completely. Beatrice giggled as we listened to Jackson sing another song from somewhere in the house. "He needs to leave today, or I will have to strangle him. Just tell him you have picked which song, so he'll go home."

"Let's get up and tell him now. I want to be alone with you. We should lock the doors so no one can visit us."

"You want us to lock everyone out so we can be alone?"

"Yes, that's what I want."

"I want you to rest today, so I'll tell Jackson he needs to leave. I don't want you disturbed. Hey, I just remembered I have a Do Not Disturb sign. I'll hang it on the front door."

"Wow, you're brilliant. Make sure the door is locked just in case they don't read the sign, and walk right in."

"Don't worry, I'll make sure. By the way, I have to go to work today." I got up and showered before going out to find Jackson. He was in the kitchen drinking a cup of coffee.

"Good morning Jackson."

"Morning. I'm heading home this morning. Have you picked a song yet?"

"Yes, but Gabby will be singing at our wedding, so you're off the hook."

"Thank the Lord. I was making myself sick just thinking about it. If you don't mind, I'll grab my bag and leave. I will see you in a few days."

"Okay, I'll see you in a few days. Stay off your leg today."

"Absolutely."

"Goodbye, Hutch.

"Bye, Jackson."

The aroma of food cooking filled the air, and got up to find Beatrice cooking breakfast. I wrapped my arms around her and held her close. She turned around and kissed me. "I have to go to work today. I will see you tonight."

"No, I still need you to stay with me. What if I need you?"

"I'll call you, but I want you to rest..."

"Hello, we're here.

"Damn, he left the door unlocked. Now what should we do?"

"Hush, she is your mother. Let her visit.

"Hello, dear."

"Mom, what are you and Hellen doing up and about this early?"

"Jackson said to come right in. We came to talk about the wedding. Where are you going?"

"I have to go to work. Come and sit down and have some coffee. I already told Hutch he has to rest today. So don't keep him up long."

We won't stay long. We need to talk to both of you."

Beatrice smiled at our moms. "Why don't both of you come to lunch with me at the hospital today?"

"We'd love to have lunch with you. That's one of the reasons I'm so happy to be back home—I get to have lunch with my daughter."

I saw Beatrice's face as she handed her mom a tissue. I hoped she didn't giggle. Her mom cried every time she was with us because she was happy to be home. Beatrice turned and looked at me and winked. Then she kissed me goodbye. "I'll see you around six thirty."

"I don't like you working," I said, frowning. Beatrice laughed as she left the room. "Hey, I was serious," I said. She walked back and kissed me again. "I love you so much. Enjoy your visit."

I turned to my mother and Beatrice's mom. "So, what do you two have so far?" It was three hours later that the moms left. It was actually a nice visit. I talked them into making brownies while we talked about the wedding. I wanted to have the wedding sooner, but they were right—this would be our only wedding, so we would make it beautiful.

We decided to use both houses, and the guest could walk from one home to the other, just like when we were growing up. All of the food would be set up in our backyard, where everyone would end up. I think our moms have everything under control. I decided to go with them when they went to have lunch with Beatrice. She was working in her office today, so we waited for her to come out.

A huge smile spread across her face when she spotted

me. "I was hoping you'd come with them, even though I told you to rest today."

"I couldn't wait until six-thirty to see you."

When we arrived at restaurant, we saw so many of the senior residents from our small-town having lunch. They kept stealing glances at Beatrice and me. I smiled as I got down on one knee. "Beatrice Price, you are the love of my life. We have been through so much together. Will you marry me and make me the happiest man on earth?"

Tears streamed down Beatrice's face as she replied, "I would love to marry the man I've been in love with for most of my life." Applause and whistles erupted around us. I pulled her into my arms as I stood up and kissed her like this was our last day on earth.

THE END

EPILOGUE

Weeks flew by, and the day of Bea and Hutch's wedding had finally arrived. The sun was shining, and the scent of fresh flowers filled the air. The guests gathered in the backyard, where both houses had been transformed into a picturesque setting. The anticipation was palpable as everyone awaited the bride's entrance.

Gabby began singing, and all heads turned to see Beatrice walking down the aisle, radiant in her white gown. As she approached Hutch, a hush fell over the crowd. It was a moment filled with love and promise—a culmination of their journey together.

The ceremony was heartfelt and intimate, with tears and laughter intermingling in the air. Vows were exchanged, sealing their commitment to each other. And when the time came, Hutch took the microphone and looked at Bea, his eyes filled with love.

"Today, I stand here not only as a groom but as a man whose life has been forever changed by the love of this incredible woman," Hutch began, his voice strong and sincere. "Beatrice, you showed me love can conquer even the deepest fears and wounds. And I am eternally grateful for the gift of your love."

The piano started playing, and we turned our heads to hear Jackson singing us a song of love. He wasn't shy now to sing in front of a crowd. He sang us a love song that had tears running down more faces than just Beatrice's. When the song ended, thunderous applause erupted. It was the perfect song for Beatrice and Hutch.

Bea looked at Hutch, tears streaming down her face, as she realized how far they had come, how they had overcome their fears and found solace and strength in each other.

In that moment, as their loved ones surrounded them, the couple knew their journey was far from over. They had conquered their demons, forged an unbreakable bond, and now embarked on a new chapter filled with adventure, love, and endless possibilities.

And so, with hearts full of gratitude and a deep sense of belonging, Hutch and Beatrice danced their way into a future brimming with happiness and the unwavering belief that, together, they could conquer anything life threw their way.

As the sun began to set, casting a warm glow over the celebration, they held each other tightly, whispering promises of forever. Their love story was far from ordinary, but it was uniquely theirs—a tale of resilience, growth, and the transformative power of love.

And as the night drew to a close, Bea and Hutch walked hand in hand into the unknown, knowing that no matter what challenges lay ahead, their love would always be their guiding light—a love that had endured, defied the odds, and blossomed into something truly extraordinary.

And so, their story continued, a love story with no ending, only new beginnings

DEAR READER.

Thank you, for your continued support. I really appreciate that you read my books.

If you can please leave me a review for this book, I would appreciate it enormously.

Your reviews allow me to get validation I need to keep going as an Indie author.

Just a moment of your time is all that is needed. I will try my best to give you the

best books I can write.

JOIN me on social media Follow me on BookBub
https://www.bookbub.com/profile/susie-mciver

NEWSLETTER SIGN UP HTTP://BIT.LY/SUSIEMCIVER_NEWSLETTER

FACEBOOK PAGE: www.facebook.com/SusieMcIverAuthor/
https://www.susiemciver.com/

KEEP READING for more of Seal Security, with the story of Jackson.

23

JACKSON

"What the hell is that noise?" I exclaimed, rushing out the back door. There, a little girl stood crying and screaming while gazing out at the waves. I knew something was wrong. Hastily I grabbed my phone and dialed nine-one-one, securing a life preserver as I ran down the beach. *What the hell is going on*? " I reached the screaming child and tried to calm her.

"Hey, sweetie, tell me what happened. She looked at me. Her face was all red from crying and screaming.

"My brother is in the water. That lady went to find him, and I can't see her."

'Fuck,' "You stay right here. Don't come near the water."

"Okay."

Diving under with each wave; I strained my eyes to see any sign of them. I knew the current must have taken them out. I don't even know if the woman found the boy. Luckily the ocean was pretty calm, which was a relief.

And then I spotted them. The woman held the boy above the water, desperately trying to revive him.

In order to avoid being hit, I had to duck as I swam up next to her, because her fist came straight at me. Taking charge, I swiftly placed the life preserver around the child, tilting his head back to begin CPR. I could feel the woman's gaze on me. Fear started to grip me as I continued my efforts, but she spoke softly to the boy, her voice as soothing as melted butter.

"Sweetheart, it's time to wake up. Come on. Your little sister needs you. Breathe now. I know you can do it." He gasped and vomited water, then took a small breath, and I heard her cry out in relief. He still hadn't gained consciousness. I kept trying to help him breathe.

Suddenly, someone touched my shoulder. I looked around, to find Ryker and Gray beside me. Equipped with floaters, and we put the boy on one. As I turned to see where the woman had gone, I noticed she was swimming away from us.

The boy started crying and vomiting, so I attended of him. I decided to speak to the woman once we taken care of the child.

Later, we provided a statement to the fire department and the police. I However the woman was nowhere to be found. As the ambulance departed the boy's parents arrived. It stopped when a crying mother wanted her crying son. So the EMTs let her join them in the ambulance, while the girl stayed with her father. The family had just moved to town and unloaded some of their things from the truck when the children took off. The parents had already reported them missing to the police.

"Did you see where the woman went?" I inquired, turning to the guys.

"What woman?"

"The woman who saved the boy. She was right beside me. I thought she would still be here on the beach," I explained approaching the little girl. "Have you seen the woman who was here?"

"Did she drown?" The little girl asked.

"I hadn't even considered that. Oh, hell, did she drown?" My impulse was to return to the water, when one of the police officers stopped me.

"Hey, Jackson."

"Yeah."

"The woman had to leave. She called us and asked us to inform you, so you wouldn't think she drowned."

"What's her name?"

"I don't know her name. Maybe dispatch will have that information."

"Could you find out for me?"

"Sure, I'll call you once I have her name."

"I looked at Gray and Ryker. "Thank God she didn't drown."

"What did she look like? This town is small. Perhaps you'll run into her again." Gray suggested.

"There was something about her that felt familiar. I only caught a few glimpses of her. She spoke to the boy, and her voice could melt butter. She was wearing a wet suit, so maybe she was surfing or diving nearby."

"So, what made her seem familiar?" Ryker asked.

"I don't know. She almost decked me when I swam up next to her and the boy. I'm sure I'll remember what it was about her that seemed familiar. In this small town there aren't many women I don't know. I wonder if she went to school with us. We better get out of these wet clothes and hit the road. Where are we headed?"

Ryker had already started removing his wet shirt and shoes off before we got to my front door. "We are going to Iran. Do you remember River Channing? He was a U.S. Army Green Beret. I heard now he was a Smoke Jumper, but he went to Iran to help a couple of friends. He hasn't been heard from since he left. His company is hiring us to find him."

"River's unit was reconnaissance. They are special operations forces. It's hard to imagine him falling into a trap if that's what they suspect," I remarked, looking at Gray with concern. Are you sure you want to come on this trip? I thought Gilly was expecting any time now."

"Two months is when the baby will be here. I have plenty of time to get River and be back home."

I looked at Gray and frowned. I was still thinking about the trap. "Even the best people can get caught in traps. Some people spend their life trying to ensnare others, finding a way to hook you until you're trapped. I'm sure that is what happened. I'll bet this whole thing was a set-up."

"I hope we can find him."

"We will. That's why they called us. Even those guys recognize the best."

∼

"Damn, it's scorching hot out here. Where are we headed?"

"We need a vehicle, and then we will figure out the direction." As we approached the desk, we inquired about renting a vehicle. The man pointed to another desk and that person handed us the keys without even asking what we wanted.

I stepped back. We all understood that meant we needed

to speak privately. "I think this is how the bad guys caught River. Should we play along so we can locate him?"

"Yeah, I say let's do it. The sooner we're out of here, the better. I can feel eyes on us."

I nodded to the guys. "I feel the same way. Okay let's get it over with." We turned around and took the keys. The man walked with us outside to the vehicle. As we got in, we prepared ourselves. Six guys approached us from behind, their guns pressed against our backs. We complied with their every command. They moved us to a larger vehicle and drove us for to a three-hours to a bullet-riddled building.

Once we got out, Gray turned to ask something and got struck on the head. I barely caught him before he hit the gravel road.

"Why did you hit him? We've done everything you asked."

"That's . Why precisely what concerns me. Why aren't you resisting?"

"We're not stupid. You're holding guns pressed into our backs. What were we supposed to do? You would have shot us before we blinked our eyes."

"I can't believe you are the feared Navy Seals everyone talks about. I'm shaking in my boots." He pushed us inside the building. I had Gray over my shoulder. I heard shouting and recognized one of the voices. I looked at Ryker to see if he recognized it too. Both of his eyebrows were raised, indicating that he did. When we reached the door, one man opened it while the other pushed us inside and slammed the door shut.

Lieutenant Carter Robinson…I thought he was dead. I wonder how long he's been here. We entered the room, and the fighting ceased momentarily as they looked at us before both started shouting.

"Shut up," I said, looking at the men. "Lieutenant, we thought you were dead?"

"Why the fuck would you think that?"

"We believed it because there were reports of your death."

He turned to look at River. "River is that what you heard?"

"That's what we were told. None of us believed it. I came here to find you."

"And instead, you end up being captured."

"The only reason I'm locked up is because it would lead me to you. I figured they'd take me straight to you."

"So that both of us could end up locked up, and now there are three more prisoners."

I held up my hand for silence. "Before you say another word, there is a camera with speakers." I dropped Gray then I checked out his wound.

Stop pushing on my head. That fucker hurts like hell. He must have hit me with a giant boulder.

"It was a steel bar he was carrying along with his gun," Ryker said, examining Gray's head.

"We're here because we knew it was a way to infiltrate this place," I whispered.

We leaned back against the same wall the camera was mounted. Then we strategized. "How many men do you think are here?"

Carter Robinson, looked at us. "Maybe seven at the same time, but we're not the only ones here. I hear a woman screaming at them all the time. She begs them to release her out so she can kill them. I think they're afraid of her. I have no idea who she is. Have any of you heard anything about a kidnapped woman?"

Gray looked at Carter. "A woman. Who could she be? We can't leave her here; they'll kill her."

"Damn it, do you know where she is?" I asked.

"I know she's down the hall from here. I hear them when they stop by and give her food. I think they throw it at her."

"Damn, we can't leave her here. Fuck. So why are we in rooms and not cells?" I asked Carter.

"Because these people despise Americans, and they want to use them for ransom. But they never release them. They take them to a place where they enslave them, and if they resist they're whipped in front of the others until they're nearly dead. Just like the Uyghurs in China."

"Why haven't we known about this place before?"

"The Lieutenant came here to investigate it, which is why I came over when he didn't get back to us."

"I wonder if they plan to take the woman there."

I don't know, but I assume that's where they take all of the Americans. These guys are vicious bastards. They enjoy inflecting pain to Americans."

"We have to have to find this place. They can't get away with this. We'll have to come back. We can't take on this trip, but we can all "Damn, we can't leave her behind. Fuck. So why are we in rooms instead of cells?" I asked Carter Robinson. "Because these people despise Americans, and they want to use them for ransom. But they never release them. They take them to a place where they enslave them, and if they resist, they're whipped in front of others until they're nearly dead."

"Why weren't we aware of this place before?"

"The Lieutenant came here to investigate it, which is why I came when he didn't return." "I wonder if they plan to take the woman there." "I don't know, but I assume that's where they take all the Americans. These guys are vicious. They enjoy inflicting pain on Americans." "We have to find this place. They can't get away with this. We'll have to come back. We can't take action on this trip, but we can gather all the necessary information for our return."

24

LEAH

That was close. Damn, I couldn't believe Jackson Barlow was there when I needed him the most. I stopped by the hospital before I left town. The little boy was still not completely recovered. I talked to Beatrice Price, or now she goes by Beatrice Campbell. I was surprised she recognized me. We didn't exactly hang out in the same groups. I lived on the wrong side of the tracks to be invited to their parties, except when Jackson invited me to his fifteenth birthday party.

I was so excited. My sister Lane and I worked on an outfit all week, and when that night came, I was ready. I planned to walk all the way to his house. I curled my hair, I even wore makeup. I borrowed a pair of shoes from my friend Amelia; she was as excited as I was.

And then we heard my dad come home. He was never quiet. He liked shouting whenever he talked, so you would quiver in your shoes. My mother was always so scared of him. I don't know why she stayed with him. He was a mean drunk son of a bitch. He beat all of us every chance he got.

"Go home, Amelia, before he sees you. Please hurry." She wasn't fast enough. He saw her in the hallway.

"What the fuck are you doing here. Don't you have a house to live in bitch!" I ran to where he had his hand up and was getting ready to swing. "Amelia, run," I shouted as his hand came down. Instead of hitting Amelia, he hit me and didn't stop.

I blacked out. My sister told me later what had happened. She said Mama and her started beating him. While I lay on the floor, unconscious, Mama stabbed him with a kitchen knife when he turned to hit her again. It went right through that evil heart of his. I was in the hospital for a long time. Mama killed herself not long after she killed that bastard. I guess she couldn't live with herself because she killed the man she thought she loved. Even though he almost killed me. Lane stayed in the custody of the State of Oregon foster care. When I left the hospital, my Mama's brother took us to live with him.

"We never even knew we had an uncle. He said he didn't know he had nieces. He lived deep in the woods and wore combat fatigues every day. He taught us everything he knew about survival. We could live in the forest and never need to buy groceries. We could swim in the ocean and stay under longer than most people. We were homeschooled; we even did college from home. We only went into town a few times a year.

Leah and I didn't mind. We loved our Uncle and didn't care if we saw another soul.

We sat around the table eating dinner. We called him uncle because that's what he was, our uncle. He kept clearing his throat. "I want to talk to you girls. I have a lot of friends in high places. You both know that. I want to run this past you two. I had a call from one of my top guys.

They are starting a new Special Operations team to hunt down terrorists and others who hate Americans. Special Operations Forces are highly trained military units specializing in unconventional warfare, counterterrorism, surveillance, and other specialized missions. You two are already highly trained for covert missions. Remember when I told you about my job and I would have to sneak into other countries?"

"Yes." I never was one to talk much. Lane said more in one day than I said in a week.

"Would the two of you want to work for the Special Forces? You will be working with me."

"Yes." We both said at the same time.

"It's not going to be easy. You may have to kill people." We nodded, and then we jumped up and down like children. That was eight years ago. Now I had to leave for Iran. Lane was able to get herself captured.

Uncle is missing, and we have a lead on a group of men holding Americans for ransom but not releasing them when they were paid. I had heard that some Navy SEALS were going to Iran. I had planned to catch a ride. As you can imagine, I was speechless when Jackson swam beside me. I thought he was a damn shark. He's lucky my fist didn't connect with his face.

Here I go again, my stupid crush on Jackson just because he invited me to his party. The whole class was probably invited. It's not like he cared if I went or not. He probably didn't even notice I didn't show up. Then I noticed the other two swimming out to us. Grayson Campbell and Ryker Malone. It was time for me to get out of here. It dawned on me to have the police tell Jackson I was alive so he wouldn't go back into the ocean hunting for me.

"Hey, Leah, are you sure you don't want to take someone with you?"

"Who would I take? River Channing and Carter Robinson are Special Ops. They and Lane are there. I'll get them out, plus the other captive Americans. We will destroy those who think they can enslave Americans."

"You might have to kill someone."

"I know, but these bastards have Uncle. I won't have any problem killing them if they've harmed my Uncle Jack."

Tony looked at me and just stared at me. All the while, I did the same to him until he looked away. "This is so important that you don't fuck this up. Don't let your emotions override your brain. I have reason to believe that there might be another Green Beret held captive there. He might be chained and beaten, but he won't be broken."

I nodded my determination fueling every fiber of my being. I had a mission to complete, and nothing would stand in my way. Who is he?"

"Faron Lightfoot."

"Faron? No way they have him. No one can keep Faron locked up."

"They can if he's beaten and chained. That's who Jack went after, at least I think that's who he went after. So now the pile grows bigger every day. I just got word three former Navy SEALS have been captured. I'm sure they did the same thing Lane did, getting caught on purpose."

"I want you to wear a disguise and brown contact lenses. Those eyes are something a man never forgets. You need to play down your beauty, or they'll keep you for themselves."

"Are you complimenting me, General?

"I would be if I was twenty years younger. I would give your man a run for his money."

"I don't have a man. And I'm not going to say any more about that. What about Lane? Do you think the disguise she wore is still on her?"

"If they haven't made her shower, she will still have it. Lighten your hair; that black is something you never forget."

"Should I wear a wig?"

"No, I have some stuff you spray on, and it will stay on until you shower."

"Don't worry about me. I'm an expert on disguises. How am I getting there?"

"A cargo plane is going there. You can catch a ride with them. You have two hours before they leave."

I jumped out of the cargo plane's door, landing in a scorching desert where there was nothing else for miles. One thing that will get you kicked out of the Special Ops is complaining. Lane and I never complained about anything. We learned years ago never to complain, or our father would give us something to complain about.

I knew I had to be this far out so no one would see me parachuting from the sky. The others are all caught and locked up. I was the one who had to reach them so we could put a stop to this enslavement. The best way to do that was to kill everyone involved. I hoped it didn't come to that.

I rolled up my parachute and buried it in the sand, ensuring it was hidden well enough that the wind wouldn't uncover it. I checked my compass and confirmed that I was headed in the right direction. I walked when the sun went down, taking advantage of the cooler night. I kept walking, part of the time I ran. When I felt the need for rest I would sleep for twenty minutes, knowing my brain would wake me up. I wasn't worried about over sleeping.

As the sun was rising, I heard a noise. It was a vehicle. Why was a vehicle driving out here in the middle of the damn desert? Luckily, my fatigues were camouflaged, so I wasn't concerned about being spotted. All the same, I lay on my stomach with my binoculars, watching the vehicle. It had to be them.

I couldn't believe how easy this was going to be. Now I followed the vehicle. It was far ahead. I knew I could find the place if I kept walking. I learned all these skills in the mountains, and then Uncle Jack took us to the desert and left us alone for a week. When he came to pick us up, we had a shelter and was cooking rattlesnake. I have never grown to like that taste.

I knew I would still had miles to go. When night fell, I spotted lights in the distance. It had to be the same old truck that transported the others to their destination. I lay down as it approached, and I could hear two men laughing as they passed. I understood their language. They thought they were so clever because they took the scared Navy Seals to enslave them.

They didn't know that the former Seals had planned all of this. I checked all the weapons I had on me. I was ready for an invasion. I knew I had to share some of these weapons with the others. I was not fond of that idea. I said a prayer for Lane that she was safe and alive.

Three hours later, I spotted the enormous building. I would have to wait until dark to infiltrate it. The place was huge. I wondered how many Americans were inside. *I hope we can save all of them.* An hour after darkness fell, I hurried toward the building, being cautious of any noise. I halted and pressed myself against the wall, not daring to breathe.

I'll have her on her knees in front of me before we are

finished with her. She'll be begging for more," one voice said.

"We're supposed to leave the women alone. I'll report you if I have to. If you're not serious about your job, leave now," another voice said.

When I recognized the voice, belonging to Uncle Jack, I nearly cried. I was certain he wanted to kill the man who had spoken about Lane like that; I wanted to kill him myself. I knew it had to be her, by the anger I heard in my uncle's voice. I waited for ten minutes before scaling the six-foot wall and, stayed next to the wall, quietly walking around to see if I could see how many people were there.

I COULDN'T SEE MUCH, except those robes hanging on a clothesline. I swiftly donned one of the robes and blended in. I spotted Jack and the man approaching my direction, so I quickly opened a nearby door to hide behind. Two men were inside. I put my finger to my lips, pretending to be one of them in my disguise. They nodded and approached the door as if to peek outside

MY VOICE WAS LOW ANYWAY, so I just lowered it more. "Be careful. They are coming this way. Move away from the door."

I surveyed the room for their weapons and noticed them leaning against the wall, including guns and knives. I didn't waste any time in conversation. I grabbed their long knives and killed them. The sight made me feel nauseous, but it was either these men or all of us. I took a deep breath and left the room.

. . .

Upon opening the next door, I found a lone man. I raised the fingers to my lips gesture but this time he smiled and shook his head. "Get on your knees," he demanded.

"Go to hell," I replied in English, swiftly stabbing him with the knife I still carried when he made a lunged for me. His eyes were in shock hearing my American accent. I examined the knife before scanning the room for another weapon. I found a longer one decorated with blue stones. Leaving the first knife lodged in the man's body.

I wanted to find out where everyone was being held, but how could I find them without the bad guys finding out who I was? I ran smack into two men as I turned a corner. Stepping back I studied them closely.

Uncle Jack realized it was me and panic washed over his face. "What are you doing? Watch where you're going. There is nothing down that hall except the new arrivals. Stay out of that area. The doors are locked, and no one can enter without the key.

"I have to count every American in this place. How many are in there?" I asked.

He glanced at the other man, who shrugged. Uncle Jack then took a key out of his pocket and handed it to me. "Are there more Americans than what is here?"

"Yes, they are at the factories. You know that."

"Of course I do. I meant besides the factories. Where are the others? I need all the papers. He wants to make sure no one has cheated him."

Uncle Jack quickly picked up on how I was leading this conversation. "Does he dare to suggest we are cheating him? Show her the papers. Who are you?"

"Never mind, I know who you are."

My brow rose, and I decided to act superior to him. "You know nothing. Give me those papers."

"Let me get them," the man said before turning away from us.

"There are three dead men here, two in one room and one in another. Did you see Lane?"

"Yes, She is with the other new arrivals. After you look at those papers, we'll leave this place."

"Why can't we grab the papers and rescue everyone? It's because they'll be waiting for us, and after they kill all the Americans—"

What are we going to do then?" I interrupted.

We'll have to plan. Memorize the best you can, and then we'll return in a few days. But before we come back, we need to plan."

"Why can't I keep the papers."

"Because they'll kill every American they hold captive."

"Okay, I'll memorize it."

"Here are the papers. You can keep them," I was busy looking through the documents to answer him. I was surprised to see how orderly the papers were. I raised my head and handed him back the papers. I don't want to keep the documents. Put them somewhere safe."

I turned and walked down the hall toward the room where the new arrivals were being held. As I inserted the key into the lock, I had a feeling they would be waiting on the other side. Pushing the door open, Lane stood there, looking at me, and screamed as I stepped inside. Her arms flew around me.

"Redbird, thank God you are okay. *I called Lane her Special Ops name.* I've been so worried about you," I said, glancing around at everyone. Suddenly I noticed Jackson, Gray, and Ryker standing there watching us. I wondered if they recognized us. I turned to River and Carter. Tonight you will leave here, stay left all the time. I have to go now. I'll leave the door unlocked,"

"Why do you have to leave? Do they suspect you?" Lane asked.

"They will when they find the three dead men. Uncle will be here he'll go with you. I'll be an hour away. I'll see you then," I replied, noticing movement and raising my hands.

"I'm sorry. Do I know you?" Jackson asked.

"I don't know, do you?" I retorted.

"Your eyes are different, and your hair, but...."

"Bye," I said cutting him off before he could say more.

Jackson
My Book

Join me on social media Follow me on BookBub
https://www.bookbub.com/profile/susie-mciver

Newsletter Sign Up http://bit.ly/SusieMcIver_Newsletter

Facebook Page: www.facebook.com/SusieMcIverAuthor/
https://www.susiemciver.com/
ARMY RANGERS SPECIAL OPS
KASH
My Book

. . .

BAND OF NAVY SEALS

KILLIAN BOOK 1
   [My Book](#)
   ROWAN BOOK 2
   [My Book](#)

ZANE BOOK 3
   [My Book](#)

STORM BOOK 4
   [My Book](#)

ASH BOOK 5
   [My Book](#)

JONAH BOOK 6
   [My Book](#)

KANE BOOK 7
   My Book

AUSTIN BOOK 8
   My Book
   LUKE
   My Book

RYES
My Book

ANGEL
    My Book
    MATT
    My Book
    JAX
    My Book
    RYAN
    My Book
    TREY
    My Book
    CONNER
    My Book

Printed in Great Britain
by Amazon